Secr
of
Magpie
Cove

BOOKS BY KENNEDY KERR

Secrets
of
Magpie
Cove

Kennedy Kerr

bookouture

Published by Bookouture in 2021

An imprint of Storyfire Ltd.
Carmelite House
50 Victoria Embankment
London EC4Y 0DZ

www.bookouture.com

ISBN: 978-1-80019-707-7
eBook ISBN: 978-1-80019-706-0

For Jean and Marjorie

We have learned that when people ask how any of us are doing, and when they really listen to the answer, with an open heart and mind, the load of grief often becomes lighter – for all of us. In being invited to share our pain, together we take the first steps toward healing.

From 'The Losses We Share' by Meghan Markle, *New York Times*, 25 November 2020

Prologue

Somewhere, at the very top of the house, a baby was crying.

Lila stood in the shadowed, high-ceilinged hallway. On the walls, the light was just good enough to make out a row of portraits in grand golden frames. She squinted to study the details. The first was an old-fashioned Italian-style painting of Madonna and child; the Virgin Mother stared at her with an inscrutable expression while breastfeeding her baby. For some reason, the painting gave Lila a sense of deep unease. She kept walking, hearing the baby in the distance.

Lila didn't recognise the house, and yet it felt somehow familiar. Why wasn't someone comforting the baby? She started to hurry along the hallway, trying to work out where the noise was coming from.

The hallway seemed to lengthen and telescope away. She walked briskly past the paintings: next was a family posed in a traditional grouping, with two King Charles spaniels sitting docile at their feet: the mother's voluminous skirts and pulled-in bodice suggested the 1700s. Then, a more modern painting of a young child reading a book. Next again, a black and white photo of a baby sleeping.

Each one made Lila feel worse: a combination of sadness and panic. She had a feeling that something terrible would happen if she didn't get to the baby in time. And, yet, something in her wanted to stop and gaze at the pictures too. There was a longing in her that rose up like a wave: to hold a child against her body, to stroke its soft cheek, to feel its warm heaviness in her arms.

As is so often the way in dreams, Lila's brain – or her soul, or whatever it is that takes us away to strange worlds every night – did not know she was dreaming. At the same time, though she knew she had never been to this house before, it felt familiar. As if this was her house and she had merely forgotten it.

It was with this feeling of strange familiarity that Lila followed more and more family and baby portraits along the hall. Finally, she reached the bottom of a long, grand set of stairs with varnished dark wood banisters and elaborately carved balusters. The carpet was a deep blood red.

Lila's unease intensified as she placed her foot onto the bottom stair; nevertheless, she started to climb.

The staircase seemed to reach up and up, out of sight, but she kept climbing. Now the staircase turned around on itself; when she reached the small landing, the cries grew louder. And yet when she started to climb again, the cries grew more distant.

Lila started opening the doors she passed, but none of them led her to the baby. The cries grew quieter. She turned around and went back down the stairs to where the cries had been loudest, but now there was nothing but silence. She felt filled with panic that she was too late. She reached for the handle of the door closest to her and opened it. In the dream, she started to sob.

Beyond the door lay jagged grey-black cliffs that plunged into a turbulent grey-blue sea. She woke, the sheets damp with her sweat and clenched between her hands, and tears running down her cheeks.

Chapter One

Lila Bridges waited anxiously outside the café. It had been closed for a month now after Serafina Lucido, its garrulous, flamboyant owner, had died.

There had been no warning. Lila couldn't say if Serafina had been suffering from a heart problem beforehand; she didn't think so, but Serafina was the type of person who wouldn't have told you if she was feeling ill. Occasionally, she took the morning off or would head upstairs to her flat if the café was quiet, but that was part of the privilege of owning your own business. Serafina had always seemed pretty robust to Lila.

Yet it was a sudden heart attack that took Serafina Lucido, and Magpie Cove – a tiny ex-fishing village on the Cornish coast – would never be the same.

Lila had been working at Serafina's, Magpie Cove's only café, for about eight months now. The first time she'd walked through the door, a little despondent and needing a coffee, she had felt the café wrap her in its warm fug of coffee and battered leather sofas. She specifically remembered that a David Bowie CD was playing in the background – Serafina had five CDs in constant rotation. Lila had drunk an exceptional coffee and admired the pot plants which hung in macramé holders from the ceiling. All around her, groups of friends, mums with kids and people with their laptops chattered amicably or looked happily lost in a world of their own. Lila had sat at the counter, aware of being alone, but Serafina had chatted to her and made her feel welcome.

The café's rough white walls – where the original stone had been painted over – were hung with paintings and drawings, all done by local artists. The front of the counter, where Lila had sat that first time, acted like a kind of local noticeboard. It was covered in business cards and leaflets or adverts for meditation lessons, local cleaners, vegetable deliveries from local farms and all manner of other goods and services. And it was true, Lila had discovered, after working there a while – if you needed a handyman or a babysitter or a recommendation for the best local restaurant, Serafina's was where you went. It was always busy, but in a comfortable way. In bad weather, the village congregated there to gossip and drink hot chocolate. In the summer, Serafina had sometimes set up a bar on the beach. In all weathers, she had thrown parties: birthdays, anniversaries, Halloween, Easter and the summer solstice, when surfers watched the sunrise over the ocean and then came back for a celebratory breakfast.

Lila looked up and down the street, but there was no sign of Serafina's son, Nathan, yet. She tapped her foot impatiently. She had a practical exam at culinary college tomorrow and she'd planned to spend the day practising her *mille-feuilles*. Not that she didn't want to know whether she still had a job or not – she definitely did – but she could have been piping cream onto perfectly crisp, buttery pastry rectangles about now; if he was late, it just meant more time she'd have to make up, baking into the night.

Serafina had been so loved in Magpie Cove. Every single one of the two hundred people in attendance at her funeral – locals, regulars at the café but also tourists who came to Magpie Cove every year – had wanted to pay their respects. Serafina's younger son James had been in Jamaica when Lila had tracked him down, finding his mobile phone number in Serafina's battered address book. Her other son Nathan lived in London. When Serafina's will had been read, it transpired she'd left her café solely to Nathan. Lila supposed that made sense: if James was usually abroad, what was he going to do with a café?

She checked her phone to see if Nathan had messaged her, but there was nothing. He had called her last week to ask if she could meet him at the café for a chat, presumably finding her details somewhere in Serafina's messy paperwork.

Lila had moved to the sleepy Cornish village of Magpie Cove from London eight months ago. For a long time, she'd thought she was happy in the capital – sure, she didn't really like her job, but who did? At least, that's what her boyfriend Tim had always said. He hated his job as an actuarial assistant in a large City firm. Lila had fallen into an IT recruitment job she was thoroughly unsuited for. She wasn't even interested in tech – or in trying to sell people on jobs she thought were boring – but a friend had got her the position and she'd stayed, not knowing what else she really wanted.

When she had first met Tim at an after-hours bar, several drinks the worse for wear – it was Lila's friend Alice's birthday. Lila had wanted to go home hours ago but didn't feel she could disappoint the birthday girl – they'd spent the night competing as to who had the worse job. Tim had claimed the moral victory at being expected to get his boss's morning bagel every day.

Yet, it eventually began to irritate Lila that Tim seemed content to complain about his job without doing anything about it. A year after they started going out, Lila had booked herself onto a beginner's bakery course at a college in central London. She'd been waiting for Alice in a café on a Saturday morning and picked up the college prospectus to leaf through while she was bored: other leaflets advertising fashion sample sales, pop-up gift shops and restaurants were distributed around the tables. She'd happened to open the prospectus on the cooking and bakery page and started reading. She'd always liked baking as a child; she'd spent hours in Aunt Joan's kitchen, learning how to rub butter into flour and carefully measuring out sugar, then marvelling at whatever fluffy, perfect creation Aunt Joan took from the oven. It had seemed like magic.

The next night, Tim had launched into his usual Sunday night I-hate-my-job depression and she'd told him that if he hated it so much, he should do something else. And he'd thrown it back in her face, saying she was exactly the same as him, which was more or less true.

She'd wanted to prove Tim wrong. She'd wanted to show him that some people really did love their jobs. That living a happy, fulfilled professional life wasn't a myth or a conspiracy, despite his many theories to the contrary. She had begun to see that Tim *adored* hating his job and complaining about it was a full-time, masochistic hobby.

So, Lila had impulsively booked herself onto the course as a kind of revenge, but the truth was that she wanted more for herself. Tim might have derived an unconscious pleasure from feeling like a victim, but she knew that wasn't who she was. The sudden realisation that unless she did something about it, she would be right where she was in another five years – in another ten years – made her feel sick.

In a way, she hadn't expected to enjoy the course as much as she did. Yes, she'd liked baking with Grandma as a kid, but that was a long time ago. Every Saturday for eight weeks Lila got out of bed, got on the tube and spent the day learning how to make bread, Chelsea buns, scones, Cornish pasties, lemon meringue pie, even pasta. She loved it.

After that, Lila knew that she wanted more, so she enrolled on a second weekend course. After she'd completed that course, her tutor told the group that she had some contacts at London restaurants who could take on a few students for work experience, if they were interested. Lila took two weeks' holiday off work and spent it doing twelve-hour days washing dishes and helping the prep cooks with hours of fruit and vegetable slicing, paring, peeling and chopping at a prestigious Michelin-star eatery.

Tim thought she was crazy. *Why spend your holidays working?* he'd asked her, but Lila had found something that made her feel alive and she wasn't going to give up on it.

For those two weeks, she couldn't wait to get out of bed every morning.

Then, one day, she'd fainted at her workstation. On the tube home, she threw up. She'd assumed it was some kind of bug.

Two months later, she'd miscarried.

Chapter Two

Lila's stomach rumbled; she'd come out to the café this morning without having breakfast. Looking at her phone again and seeing there was still no message, she dashed across the road and pushed open the door to Maude's Fine Buns, which took up half of one of the narrow shopfronts on the street that had once been Victorian terraced houses.

'Morning, my love. What can I get yer?'

Maude, the owner of the bakery, was a rotund woman in her early forties, her brown hair a long plait which was pinned around her head. She wore a baby-pink apron with the name of the shop sewn on it in white script. Lila had often joked with her that the name of the shop should be Maude's Fine Baps if Maude was going to persist on displaying it across her ample bosom.

'Hi, Maude. Bacon roll, thanks.'

'Right you are. Lovely day…' Maude cast an eye out of the bakery window. 'How's things?'

'All right. I'm supposed to be meeting Serafina's son. He's telling me what he wants to do with the café, apparently.' Lila pulled at a loose thread on the cuff of her cardigan.

'Keep it open, I hope.' Maude handed her a soft white roll filled with salty, mouth-watering bacon and tomato sauce; Lila was a regular. She'd often pop in on the days she wasn't working at the café and pick up a bacon or sausage roll for breakfast and a coffee – Maude's was just as good as the thick, chocolatey coffee they served at the café – and take it down to the beach to eat, if it was a bright morning.

Lila loved the mornings in Magpie Cove. There was nothing nicer than waking up at six or seven, pulling on a sweatshirt and jeans and running down to the beach to watch the tide go out and expose the white sand that lay beyond the pebbly part of the cove.

She hadn't known she was pregnant before the miscarriage. Her periods weren't that regular anyway and after a couple of weeks of nausea she felt more or less all right again, so when it came, she had at first put the cramps down to a heavy period. Then, when it was clear that wasn't what it was, she had run to the bathroom and sat on the toilet, staring at the bathroom door in shock for what seemed like hours, though it must have only been minutes. It had been a child.

After some time had passed, she'd made her way – uncomfortably, a towel wedged between her legs – to her phone and called the ambulance.

Only when the paramedic arrived at the flat had she cried.

Tim hadn't said much that was helpful. He'd asked her, confused, *wasn't she on the pill? How had it happened?* When she hadn't been able to explain, he'd hugged her awkwardly and told her it was probably for the best.

Two weeks after it happened – when she could more or less move around as normal again – Alice helped her pack. Lila was traumatised by the miscarriage, but above all, she didn't want to have Tim's baby. Once she'd realised that – as she lay on their bed with a hot water bottle on her back while he was out at the pub – all the decisions were easy. She gave in her notice at the IT recruitment company. She had a few weeks of leave she hadn't taken and some savings in the bank.

Lila went to stay with her Aunt Joan in Plymouth, not knowing what she'd do next, but knowing she couldn't stay in London anymore. She just couldn't. Nothing good had happened there, apart from learning to cook, and she could do that anywhere.

The one upside of Lila's recruitment job was that the pay was decent, and she'd been saving up for a deposit on a house for years. She was still a long way from that, but seeing as she'd pretty much said goodbye to the city for now, it was time to make different plans.

'All goin' well? The course?' Maude had become a bit of a mentor to Lila since she'd been living in Magpie Cove: helping her perfect her puff pastry one rainy Sunday; another day they'd spent hours making choux pastry and filling what seemed like thousands of profiteroles with crème patissiere for a birthday party Maude was catering. Occasionally she needed a hand, and it was good experience for Lila. Maude was a little older than Lila, but not that much – it was like being friends with a school friend's older sister, had she had any close friends at school.

'Yeah. It's great.'

Lila had a favourite rock to sit on towards the back of the cove, where she ate her bacon rolls on weekend mornings and gazed out at the sea – when the weather was good, anyway. On the other side of the rock promontory that ran behind her spot, you could see the roofs of a couple of houses. There was only one house on the beach, though; it had been renovated a year or so ago. Serafina had told her that before then, it had been a bit of a ruin. The woman who lived there with her family, Mara, had worked at the café before Lila. They'd had a few polite chats but nothing significant: Mara wrote children's books and Lila thought she and her husband – or boyfriend, Lila wasn't sure – might be involved in property renovation too.

On one of her mornings staring at the sea, Lila had realised that she and Tim had been what women's magazines called *co-dependent*. Tim had loved her for as long as she supported his need to resent his job – and his life, really – by hating her own. When that changed, their relationship had changed – the miscarriage hadn't even been what had truly ended it. If she was honest, it was over on the day she booked herself onto that first eight-week cooking course.

At the time, Alice had said, *He's jealous of you, babes. You're finally doing something that makes you happy and he's scared.* But Lila hadn't wanted to see it then. It had taken the miscarriage for Lila to see that Tim didn't really love her in the way that she wanted to be loved. And that she didn't love him either.

One day, as she lay despondently on Aunt Joan's sofa, flicking through the local newspaper, she'd seen an advertisement for a well-known catering college in St Ives, Cornwall. They offered the diploma Lila had been considering doing in London, but at the time she'd rejected the idea because she would have had to leave her job. Now that had happened, she was free as a bird. What was stopping her?

Lila was so used to thinking the worst – a habit picked up from Tim – that something in her hadn't really thought it was possible she could go to college and learn to cook.

She told Alice about the course on the phone and found herself making assumptions – that it would be too expensive, that she wasn't experienced enough to be accepted, that she wasn't good enough, that she was too old to start something new. Fortunately, Alice had an answer for everything. *You're only thirty-three. You can stay with your auntie while you find your feet. You've got the money, and you're great at cakes. I'll come and visit.*

When Lila was up to it, Aunt Joan had driven them both over to St Ives to visit the college and have lunch. Lila had fallen a little bit in love with St Ives with its bustling harbour, gourmet restaurants and beautiful, quaint cobbled streets. It was a million miles away from the smog and the crowded streets of London which she had always felt were so impersonal. And the college was amazing: she'd be learning how to make restaurant-grade patisserie. They even had visiting guest chefs from around the world. Graduates from the course, the friendly tutor had told her, typically ended up working in private catering or in restaurants internationally.

Talking to the students on the course at the college had decided her. Lila had realised that every single one of them had an excited glow about them when they talked about baking and what they were learning. That was what she wanted for herself. That glow.

'D'you think there's a chance he won't want to keep the café open, like?' Maude turned to serve a tourist some Cornish pasties. Lila stepped aside while Maude took the money and put the flaky, warm golden pastries into a pink paper bag.

'I don't know. I don't know anything about him, except he worked at a bank. Doesn't exactly have much experience of running a café, I'm guessing.' Lila kept her eyes on the street, waiting for him to arrive.

She hadn't told Maude about the miscarriage, or anyone in Magpie Cove. Not even Serafina, who was – had been, she corrected herself – one of the kindest people she'd ever met.

Lila felt protective of her experience. If she didn't talk about it, she could pretend it hadn't happened. Life was good now. It was nice to chat about inconsequential things with her neighbours, to swap pleasantries with customers in the café, to gossip with Maude and talk about pastry and cake mixes and different kinds of ganache. She didn't want to discuss the thing that still woke her up at night, sweating, the same nightmare over and over again. She didn't want to talk about how she'd felt when she'd had to go to hospital on her own in the ambulance: *sometimes, your body just needs a bit of help – we've got to make sure everything's okay with you*, the paramedic had said to her, so kindly, it made her cry all over again. She certainly didn't want to tell anyone that Tim hadn't been able to take a day off work to pick her up when it was time to come home.

Lila had chosen Magpie Cove as a base while she was studying because the rents were significantly cheaper than St Ives. The course fees had taken up a good amount of her nest egg, so although it meant a drive to college a few times a week, it was still more economical. With a part time job, if she was careful, she could make it to the end of the course and still have a little bit over to tide her through whatever came next. It was a balancing act, though, which meant that helping Maude with the occasional catering job was a welcome source of extra cash.

'Nathan don't have much experience of Magpie Cove either. Not for years anyway,' Maude added conspiratorially when the tourist had left. 'Serafina lived here for years, even when the boys was little. They'd have grown up here. But she said to me once or twice, it'd been too long since either of 'em visited. That James, he was off travellin' the world. An' Nathan, maybe he thought he were too good for Magpie Cove.' Maude pursed her lips. 'Not that I'm one to gossip, my love.'

'Of course.' Lila grinned at her friend, knowing that the rumour mill in Magpie Cove ran hot on even the smallest amount of fuel. That was another reason she'd held back talking about the miscarriage. She didn't want to be gossiped about. She didn't want sympathetic looks and intrusive questions and *never-mind-dearys* from well-meaning customers. She just wanted to get on with her life.

Also, there was still a stigma attached to miscarriage, though she didn't understand why. She'd researched the facts: though it was hard to be exact, it happened in something like 15 to 20 per cent of all pregnancies. She'd read the leaflet the nurse had given her in hospital: she knew it was *perfectly normal,* she knew it was *okay to grieve*, and the nurse had held her hand and told her brightly that she would be absolutely fine and go on to have plenty of babies if she wanted to.

But reading about something in a leaflet wasn't really the same as experiencing it, and Lila – someone who had never particularly thought about having children – now worried that she wouldn't be able to have one. What if that had been it? Her one chance? And she'd blown it – by, what? Working too hard? Not being in love with Tim? Maybe those things affected a miscarriage, somehow? The nurse had assured her there was no particular cause – sometimes you could have a miscarriage because of a specific physical issue, but many times it happened for no reason at all. Yet Lila couldn't get it out of her head – what if she'd done something to make it happen? Had she unconsciously sabotaged herself? Or was it just bad luck? *In which case, when will the good luck start?* she wondered. Some good luck would be good about now.

'Speak o' the devil. He waiting for you, is he?'

Lila turned around and peered through the glass. She recognised Nathan, Serafina's older son, from the funeral. Time to stop thinking about the past and focus on the present, at least temporarily. She purposefully put those thoughts away and concentrated on the feeling of her feet on the ground. *This is now. You are here,* she thought to herself. *Be present.*

'Yes, he is.' She swallowed the last of the bacon roll and watched the neat, attractive young man standing outside Serafina's Café, tapping his phone.

At the funeral, James, the other brother, had seemed open and chatty, but Nathan had glowered at everyone and said as little as possible. Of course, he was mourning his mother, and Lila understood that everyone reacted differently to such a deep loss. But he'd put everyone's backs up that day with his manner, and Lila couldn't help but wonder whether he was always like that. Lila also distinctly remembered noticing that James's brown suit didn't fit him that well; in fact, he'd confessed to her that he'd had to buy it at a second-hand shop in Truro on his way to Magpie Cove because he didn't own a suit at all. Nathan, by comparison, looked like an Armani model in a sleek black suit and shiny, expensive-looking black shoes.

'Aren't you going to go?' Maude asked, just as a message flashed up on Lila's phone.

I'm at the café. Waiting for you. Please let me know if there has been a delay. Nathan.

'Well, here goes nothing.' Lila took a deep breath and arranged a pleasant smile on her face. 'Do I look like the model employee?' She batted her eyes at Maude. She had always been able to act when she felt down. It was easy to laugh along and be pleasant. You could save your tears for when you were alone: no one wanted to see that.

'Gorgeous. Good luck!' Maude waved a bread knife at her. 'Knock him dead.'

Chapter Three

'Sorry. I was just talking to my friend in the bakery opposite.' Lila pointed at Maude's place.

Nathan's gaze flickered over to the bakery and back to Lila.

'I thought I was going to be late. I couldn't work out where to park.' He must have caught her frown, because he added, 'It's been a long time since I was here. You forget.'

'Yeah. There are some places to park, but you have to know where they are to avoid finding yourself down a narrow lane with no way out.' She held out her hand for his, to shake it. 'Lila Bridges.'

'Nathan DaCosta. Thanks for coming.' He spoke formally, as if they were about to go into a shareholder meeting. Today he wore expensive-looking, tailored dark-grey wool trousers and a white shirt which looked as if it had come from one of those exclusive places where City boys had their shirts made and monogrammed for them. He wasn't wearing a tie. Lila wondered if that was his version of casual.

'Welcome. Though it's not your first time here, of course…' She didn't want to pry, but she was curious as to why Nathan hadn't visited Serafina in the eight months Lila had been working at the café. According to Maude, it had been a lot longer than that, too.

'No,' he replied neutrally. Lila waited for him to say something more, but he gave her a tight smile and gestured towards the café door. *A closed book,* she thought. *Fair enough.* Lila understood that sometimes it was easier that way. 'Shall we?'

In contrast to Nathan's tailored look, Lila wore her favourite jeans with holes in the knees, trainers and a yellow cardigan with frayed cuffs. Her short, curly red hair hadn't even been brushed recently: she tended to rake her fingers through it on days when she wasn't working. When she was at Serafina's, she set it in rollers the night before and wore one of her many vintage tea dresses. She liked dressing up for the café or for college, but when she was home, she gave herself permission to be less finished.

Nathan shook out Serafina's set of keys from his pocket, where they'd been ruining the line of his perfectly pressed trousers. Lila had a moment of sadness, seeing the keys – Nathan hadn't taken off any of Serafina's ridiculous keyrings, which included a large rainbow-coloured fluffy bunny, a pink skull on a chain and a slice of citrine crystal for good luck and to attract money. He tried the first key in the lock; it half turned, but the door didn't give.

'It's the deadlock first.' Lila pointed to the long key which opened the bottom lock. 'The top one's a bit of a funny one. You have to—'

'I'm sure I'll manage,' Nathan interrupted her, jabbing the key she'd pointed to in the deadlock and turning it. 'Is there an alarm system?'

'No. She kept thinking about it, but she never got around to it.'

'Why am I not surprised?' he muttered.

Lila watched as he tried the top key again with no luck. 'Do you want me to do it? You've got to push the door at the same time…' She reached for the keys and he glared at her.

'I think I can open a bloody door, okay?' he muttered again. She stood back.

'Sure. Go ahead.' *Typical man,* she thought. *No – typical City boy.*

Apart from Maude's Fine Buns and Serafina's, the high street consisted of a small florist that had just opened, an antique shop, the Shipwreck and Smuggling Museum, an art gallery and a local butcher. You got to the beach by walking through a narrow alley between Maude's Fine Buns and the butcher next door. Lila was still trying to formulate the perfect joke about smuggling sausages between Maude's Fine Buns, but she didn't quite have it yet.

At the other end of the street, there was another café, but Lila had never seen it open. The drab décor through the grimy window was covered in dust, and the menu on the door was yellowing with age. Lila wondered who even owned it. Serafina must have known. Lila's heart tugged at the thought she wouldn't see her friend again. They hadn't known each other that long, but to Lila, Serafina had been a ray of light at a time when her world was dark.

Magpie Cove was an odd sort of place. Some businesses, like Serafina's, seemed to thrive, but it was hard making a living for most. The tiny beachside village wasn't like upscale, busy St Ives where you could find oyster restaurants, art galleries, pottery shops and independent fashion boutiques doing a roaring trade all year round with locals and tourists. There were fudge shops, postcard kiosks and shops selling shells, buckets and spades, as well.

What if Nathan decided to sell the café? She didn't want to go back to London, but there were precious few other local jobs. She could probably find something in St Ives, but she'd have to continue to live in Magpie Cove.

Magpie Cove tended to be quiet for most of the season. There wasn't much to attract tourists, though the sandy cove was popular with small groups of surfers. The village also occasionally hosted artists who came for the good light, cheap rent and the proximity to the galleries in St Ives. Serafina's was a refuge for locals and artists alike.

Nathan sat down at one of the tables and motioned to her to join him.

'Shall I make some coffee?' Lila felt the need for something to wash down the bacon roll she'd just devoured.

'Perhaps in a moment. I want to talk to you first.' Nathan placed a dark-brown leather briefcase on the table and opened it with a click. 'Now. I understand you've been working here… six months?' He looked up from a sheaf of papers at her.

'Eight.'

'And you were Mum's only employee?'

'Yes,' Lila confirmed.

'How was business? From your point of view?' He looked around at the café walls, hung with paintings and canvases from local artists. 'And did this stuff actually sell? Or was Mum just providing some kind of free gallery space for the local hippies?'

'Business was good, as far as I could tell. We were always busy. Lots of regulars and a fair bit of passing trade. Surfers, sometimes there's an art fair nearby and we get a bit of that custom. Sometimes tourists exploring out from St Ives.'

Nathan nodded. 'And the art?'

'We sold stuff sometimes. But I think Serafina liked having it here – kind of like a gallery space, yeah. But when a lot of your customers are local artists, it's kind of a nice thing to do, isn't it? For the community?'

'For the *community*.' Nathan rolled his eyes. 'The number of times I heard that growing up…'

'You make it sound like a bad thing.' Lila raised an eyebrow.

Nathan picked up a pen and didn't answer. *Cold fish*, she thought. She had to admit he was good-looking, but he seemed so closed off – almost like he was afraid to have a personality. She felt like telling him he didn't have to be so formal, that it was only Magpie Cove, but she'd only just met the man. Plus, he was her new boss. Maybe.

There was a jingle of bells as the door was pushed open. Lila looked up to say, *We're closed*, and spotted two of Serafina's regulars, Cyd and Betty, peering in.

'I saw you sitting there with the lights on and wondered if you were open, my love.' Cyd breathed heavily, her fingers tight around the tartan shopping trolley she took everywhere.

'Oh. Hi, ladies.' Lila got up and walked over to the door. 'I'm afraid we're not. Just having a meeting.'

The café usually opened early three times a week for a group of Serafina's elderly customers who came in for breakfast around eight thirty. They'd been coming on Monday, Wednesday and Friday mornings for years; Lila thought it pretty likely that Serafina hadn't changed the senior citizen early bird special price for all that time, either, which was ridiculously cheap. The bottomless cups of tea and coffee and towering plates of poached eggs, spinach on toast and bacon butties Serafina and Lila made for Cyd, Betty, Eric and Rovina and the rest of Magpie Cove's senior citizens definitely cost Serafina more than the couple of pounds she charged her pensioners. When Lila had brought it up once, Serafina had looked cagey about the money.

'Look, Lil. Way I see it, it's the least I can do. Rovina lost her whole family when she was eight – bombed in World War Two, she was the only one left. She had to go into an orphanage, poor lamb. She's never had anyone to look after her. Eric's a retired policeman, bless his heart, he was the bobby on the beat around Magpie Cove for as long as I can remember. Cyd used to run the library. Her legs aren't so good these days. Betty's on her second heart bypass. Bit of bacon and a cuppa here and at least I know she's eating *something*. It's not like any of them have much in the cupboard at home,' she'd explained. Lila had understood then that she wasn't to mention to Betty, Eric and the rest the fact that the cost of breakfast hadn't risen in fifteen years – and she never did.

'I told you, ye old biddy!' Betty waved her walking stick at her friend. 'Says it's closed. Sorry to have troubled you, dear. Nice to see you, though.'

'It's nice to see you too.' Lila frowned and looked back at Nathan. 'It's just that—'

'Ooh, is that Nathan?' Betty interrupted her and pushed past Lila into the café. 'As I live and breathe! You're just like your mother!'

Nathan stood up and came over, arranging a polite expression on his face.

'Nathan DaCosta.' He held out his hand formally, as if Cyd and Betty weren't a pair of elderly gossips but two corporate CEOs. Lila couldn't work out if this was out of politeness or just that he didn't know how to talk to people any other way.

'Ooh, he's handsome, isn't he, Cyd?' Betty crooned. 'Puts me in mind of a young Cat Stevens.'

Lila had to suppress a laugh. Was that a blush she detected on Nathan's cheeks?

'Well, nice to meet you, I'm sure.' Cyd had rolled in, clutching her shopping trolley for support. 'But if I don't get back soon, my varicose veins are goin' to give me hell. Come on, Bet.'

Lila felt terrible. Neither Cyd nor Betty were that good on their feet anymore and usually they'd have had breakfast and a good sit down to fuel them up to make the walk home. Cyd and Betty lived together in a house quite a few streets away; Magpie Cove's cobbled streets weren't exactly ideal for pensioners to begin with. They'd been resisting sheltered housing for years. *Not while I've got all me marbles,* Betty had once exclaimed. *If I can still clean me own kitchen, I'm stayin' at home with Cyd.*

'Umm, Nathan, can I have a word?' Lila murmured; he nodded. 'Ladies, take a seat for a minute.' Lila pointed them to the nearest table. 'I'll be right back.'

Lila led Nathan behind the counter as the women let themselves in and made their way shakily to a table.

'Look. The thing is, they normally come in for breakfast a few times a week, and they haven't been able to for a month. Since they're here, can I make them something? We've probably got bread in the freezer, there's tins of beans. Probably some frozen pastries.' Lila looked over at the table where Cyd was carefully lowering herself into a chair with Betty's help.

'Umm… well, I hadn't really planned for this,' Nathan muttered. 'We're not technically open. In terms of health and safety…'

'I know. But they're so frail,' Lila pleaded in a low voice – she wouldn't want to let Cyd and Betty hear. They would never want to think of themselves as needing charity.

'Okay, I guess so. I wouldn't want to be responsible for turning a couple of elderly women out on the street,' Nathan conceded.

'Great. Thanks – I really appreciate it. Let me go and tell them, okay?' Lila pulled an apron out of a drawer and tied it around her waist. 'We can still talk while they're here.'

'Sure.' Nathan sat on one of the stools at the counter and looked at his phone.

'All right, ladies. How does beans on toast and a cup of tea sound?' Lila went back to Cyd and Betty and laid out some cutlery and napkins on the table. 'You'll have to excuse us, we weren't planning to have anyone here today.'

'I thought you weren't open!' Betty exclaimed, a twinkle in her eye. 'We couldn't possibly take advantage!'

'She's lyin'. We hoped you'd take pity on us if you were in. Like two stray cats. Only with support hose.' Cyd shot Betty an arch stare.

Betty sniffed. 'Speak for yourself. I still wear a girdle an' stockings.'

'Well, I can't send you home without feeding you. Serafina would be very disappointed,' Lila interrupted. 'I might be able to add in a *pain au chocolat* as well. It's on the house,' she whispered. She'd already decided she would pay for Cyd and Betty's food, even though she hadn't been paid for a month. Both women looked gaunt: she could cope with giving Nathan a few pounds if she had to.

'Oh, well, if you insist, my love.' Cyd patted Lila's arm affectionately. 'That'd be lovely. I must admit 'tis a relief to sit down. These streets seem to get steeper every week.'

'How have you been, anyway?' Lila picked up pepper and salt shakers from a neighbouring table: there were none where Cyd and Betty sat.

After Serafina had died, Lila had had to close the café pretty quickly, and though she'd cleaned up and given away all the perishable food that was in the fridge and on the counter – the cakes, fruit and buns – now she could see there was lots that needed to be done. The windows hadn't been washed: usually the sun streamed through them in the morning, but at the moment they were dim and dirty. The whole place needed a dust and the surfaces needed to be cleaned down too.

'Bearin' up, maid. Bearin' up. We've missed our breakfasts, though, I must say. Meals on Wheels has got even worse. Lucky if we get a pork chop twice a week, we are.' Betty sighed. 'Don't get old, my love, is my advice.'

'Even worse?' Lila moved the shopping trolley to one side so it was by the wall. 'I thought you were supposed to get proper meals delivered every day. Isn't it run by the council?'

'Aye, but they changed the people what make the food, they said. Budget cuts, I'll wager.' Cyd rolled her eyes. 'Hardly edible. Watery soup. Cold when it comes, usually. D'you reckon that

nice young man'll open the café again soon? We're half starvin'
without it.'

Lila looked back at Nathan, who was still tapping away at
his phone.

'I don't know,' she replied, honestly. 'But I'll do everything I
can to persuade him. I promise.'

Chapter Four

'So. As you might know, Mum left the management of the café and her property interests to me, though James and I co-own everything,' Nathan explained when Lila finally sat down. She'd managed to find beans, made toast and put the frozen *pains au chocolat* in the oven to bake. Cyd and Betty were happily drinking tea and demolishing their breakfasts a few tables away.

'I see.' Lila watched his face as he talked; it was completely expressionless. She wondered if he had ever run around as a kid, made faces, laughed and sang. She just couldn't imagine it at all.

'I'm going to be selling Mum's flat above the café, and I've been wondering whether to keep the café open or do something else with the space,' he added.

'Right…' She took a deep breath. 'The thing is, I need to know if I still have a job,' she explained. 'Because if I don't, I need to find something else. I've got to stay in Cornwall to finish my patisserie course; I've got four months left, and then there's no guarantee I'd find a patisserie job straightaway. Working at the café and living in Magpie Cove means I can afford to carry on with it. Serafina – your mum – told me I could stay here as long as I needed to.'

'I see. So, you… bake?' He met her eyes with his cool stare. His eyes were soft-lashed and a deep brown. Lila remembered Serafina telling her that her own family, the Lucidos, were originally Spanish and her husband, Trevor, had been Jamaican. Both Nathan and James had light brown skin and black hair, and though James had locs, Nathan's hair had the more Spanish, voluptuous, thicker curl on the top, where it was slightly longer than its smooth and perfectly barbered back and sides.

By the time Lila had started working at the café, Serafina's hair was white, but Lila had seen pictures of her when she was younger and she'd had long, thick dark hair which hung in perfect ringlets. Nathan was very like her, with his slightly pouty mouth and large, expressive eyes. Yet they couldn't be more different, Lila thought. Nathan had none of his mother's warmth.

'Yes. Patisserie.'

'That's not baking?'

'It's like the difference between a hedge fund and a child's savings account,' she countered. 'If I was to speak your language.'

'Touché.' A glimmer of a smile played around his lips. 'So, what kind of things are you learning? Why patisserie? And why here?' He sat back in his chair and folded his arms on his chest.

'Why are you interested?' She sat forward. 'Can't you just tell me if I have a job? That's all I really want to know.'

'I don't know if I'm going to keep the café open yet, but I will let you know by the end of next week,' he said. 'I'm exploring options. But I will pay you until I make a decision. It's only fair.'

'Right. But that still kind of leaves me in limbo as to whether I need to get a new job or not,' she explained patiently; perhaps Nathan had never been in a situation like this before – not knowing if he had a job or not. He'd probably gone from some posh school to a Fortune 500 company and never looked back.

'I can't help that.' He shrugged. 'You were telling me about the patisserie?'

Just how dense is he? Lila stared in disbelief. He must have correctly interpreted her thoughts, because he added an explanation.

'I'm considering some other options for the café, like private catering. Supper clubs, for instance. If you're a pastry chef, it would be useful to know what you can do.'

'Oh…' Lila felt put on the back foot; working in the café was great, but when she graduated from college, private catering was high on her list. She loved the idea of creating top-notch desserts for parties, weddings, maybe even companies. She could develop her own specialities: she loved doing twists on French classics, like her lime, lemongrass and coconut eclairs. 'What are you saying? You'd give me a job doing that?'

'It's too soon to tell. But I'd like to know if one of my employees has a key skill for the business going forward.'

'You should talk to Maude, over the road. She caters for parties—'

'Maybe. But I don't employ Maude, I employ you. So, tell me about you. Anyway, I bet Maude's got enough on her hands with her Fine Buns.' A hint of a grin again, and then it was gone. Lila wasn't sure if he'd actually made a joke or not.

'Well, I started the course last year. It's a Level 3 Diploma in Patisserie and Confectionery. I did some short courses while I was still living in London, as well as doing work experience at a couple of restaurants. When I moved to Cornwall, I started the diploma.'

'You lived in London?'

'Yeah. I went there for university and stayed. Seven years, more or less.'

'So you studied… cooking… at university?'

'Law. Didn't suit me, though. Dropped out.'

'Oh.' He sat back, looking unimpressed. 'What did you do after that?'

'IT Recruitment.'

'Not for you either?'

'Not really.' Lila felt as though he was criticising her.

'So you moved here…'

'Correct.' She stared back at him, meeting his gaze.

'Why Cornwall?' he persisted.

'Fancied a change.' She wasn't going to tell him the real story. Why would she?

The smell of cooking pastry filled the air and Lila remembered the *pains au chocolat* in the oven. 'One minute.' She got up, opened the oven and took out the tray. She'd made four: she put two onto plates and took them over to Cyd and Betty, and, when she was back at the counter, placed the other two on separate side plates and pushed them across. 'Thought I might as well make an extra couple for us,' she mumbled.

'You could have asked before you wasted even more of my profits.' His face was expressionless again.

'Are you kidding me? It's a couple of frozen pastries. I was just trying to be nice.' Lila was starting to lose her temper. 'And if you think a couple of cups of tea and a bit of beans on toast for two elderly customers that have been coming here for fifteen years or more is a waste, then I'm not sure I want to work for you anyway.' She untied her apron and flung it onto the counter. There was just something in his manner that wound her up the wrong way, and she felt very protective of Cyd and Betty, particularly now that Serafina wasn't around. Somehow, Lila knew that Serafina would expect her to make sure they were all right. If Nathan didn't have any compassion for his elders – or any bloody *respect,* come to that – then he could bloody well bugger off.

'Whoa. I was joking!' Nathan stared at her, alarmed at her sudden temper. 'Calm down. Of course, I don't care about a few *pains au chocolat.*'

'Oh.' Lila felt instantly foolish. 'It's just that… the way you said it… you're very serious. How was I supposed to know that was a joke?'

'Sorry. I have an odd sense of humour.' He looked away, embarrassed.

'If it was a joke, it wasn't funny,' Lila muttered. 'Cyd and Betty rely on Meals on Wheels and the café. Look at them. They're skin and bone.'

Nathan stared at the elderly ladies for a few moments.

'I'm sorry, I didn't know,' he said, quietly. 'I… I suppose I don't think about people not having enough to eat.'

'I don't suppose you do.' Lila gave him a very obvious look up and down to make sure he knew that she could see his clothes probably cost more than Cyd and Betty's annual fuel bill. 'But times are hard for a lot of people here.'

'Sorry,' he repeated, and stood up. 'Look. Can you close up when Cyd and Betty are ready to go? I've got to be in St Ives in half an hour and I'm not going to make it unless I go now. I'll be in touch when I've decided about the café, okay? I promise I'll let you know as soon as I can.'

'All right.' Lila looked up, discomfited. He wasn't even going to stay to the end of the meeting? It seemed odd, his suddenly rushing off.

He dropped the café keys onto the counter and Lila put them into her jeans pocket. After Serafina had died, she'd had to use the spare set Serafina had given her for emergencies to get in the café and sort everything out, but she hadn't thought to bring them with her today. She thought it was entirely likely that she'd probably just lost any chance she might have had of keeping her job, even if Nathan kept the café open, but she couldn't help her outburst. Maybe she'd made him uncomfortable, she didn't know.

'How will I get them back to you? The keys?' She pointed at them. 'I've got a spare set at home too, if you want them.'

'Oh, right. Um. Text me your address and I'll come and get them later.' He gave her a quick smile. He looked nice when he smiled, and she couldn't imagine why he didn't do it more often. He *was* like a young Cat Stevens, Lila observed; Aunt Joan had one of his flower power folky albums with his face on it, so she could see the resemblance.

'Okay,' she replied, smiling back shyly.

'See you, then.' He looked like he was going to say something more, but then turned and made his way out of the café. 'Ladies.' He nodded to Cyd and Betty formally, and left. Lila thought he would have tipped his hat to them if he'd been wearing one.

Once he was gone, Lila cleared Cyd and Betty's plates, happy – but also sad – to see that the pensioners had demolished everything. It bothered Lila, what Betty had said about Meals on Wheels. She could see they were both getting more frail.

'Well, my maid, thankee for feedin' a couple of old scroungers.' Betty patted the back of Lila's hand as she wiped the table.

'You're welcome. Look, I'll walk you home if you give me ten minutes to clear up,' Lila offered.

'You don't have to, but 'tis always nice to have company.' Cyd grinned. 'And gives me another ten minutes sittin', so I'm not complainin'.'

'Deal.'

Lila took the plates back to the kitchen and washed them up by hand, standing them on the drainer to dry. She double checked the fridge to make sure nothing perishable was in it, and put the *pain au chocolat* bag back in the freezer.

There was still a lot of food in there, and Lila stared at it thoughtfully.

It was unlikely that Nathan knew exactly what was there – Serafina wasn't a great record-keeper and Lila seriously doubted that she had a tally of every sausage and frozen garlic baguette. If the café didn't even open again, what would happen to that food? She suspected it would be thrown away.

Lila looked over at Cyd and Betty.

What if it wasn't thrown away – but given to some people that needed it?

Lila stood behind the counter, lost in thought. If she gave some of the food to Cyd and Betty, was it stealing?

She'd have to mention it to Nathan. It was only right.

But the idea that he might say no – or that he might tell her to bring the food back – filled her with trepidation. If she just took the food now, who would know? Wasn't it essentially the same as providing incredibly cheap breakfasts in the café? They were already more or less giving the food away…

If the café's closing, then what have I got to lose? Lila thought. *And, if I'm honest, I don't feel particularly bad about taking food from Mr Hoity Toity.* He had been so rude to her.

Without letting herself think about it any more deeply, she grabbed a packet of sausages, two packets of bacon, a bag of garlic baguettes and a bag of chicken breasts and slid them into one of the paper carrier bags which were stacked under the counter.

She carried the bag over to the table and handed it to Betty.

'Doggy bag.' She winked. 'Have you got room in the shopping trolley?'

'What's this?' Betty peered into the bag. 'What're you up to, you naughty so-and-so?'

'Just a few bits. Honestly, I'm not sure if Nathan's going to keep the café open at all, so it may as well not go to waste.' Lila folded the top of the bag over and placed it inside Cyd's tartan shopping trolley.

'Oh, we can't accept that, my love.' Cyd tried to pull the bag out, but Lila gently unhooked her hand from the paper bag.

'Please. I don't like the thought of you going without. And if the café closes, then I'll find some other solution for you. Think of it as a gift from me.'

Cyd sighed theatrically.

'Well, never let it be said I looked a gift horse in the mouth when it tried to give me a frozen bit o' bacon.' She leaned forward carefully and enveloped Lila in a hug. Lila could feel Cyd's ribs as she hugged her back gently. 'Thankee, maid.'

'It's nothing.' Lila helped them on with their coats. Betty tried to leave some money on the table, but Lila picked it up and gave it back to her.

'Don't be silly. We're not open, so this never happened,' she tutted.

'Ooh, she's a proud mare, this one.' Betty laughed. 'Well, in that case I will say please and thank you for our lovely breakfast and God bless yer for takin' pity on us, pathetic as we are.'

'You're not pathetic.' Lila held out her arm for Cyd. She escorted both women out of the door and locked up behind them.

As she gazed into the café from outside, Lila's hand hesitated on the doorknob. It was just a few sausages and a bit of chicken, and she knew she would have had Serafina's blessing to help Cyd and Betty. So why did she suddenly feel so guilty?

Chapter Five

No one ever came up to the cliff path if it was bad weather, so when Lila woke to the sound of rain outside her window, she knew she'd have Magpie Point to herself.

The dream clung to her eyelashes; she sat up and wiped her eyes blearily. It was regular, a few times a month since she'd had the miscarriage. The same dream, being in the unfamiliar house, the baby crying somewhere in the distance. The setting of the dream itself was spooky, but nothing terrible ever happened, apart from the feeling. As the dream progressed, the terrible feeling that the baby would go silent, and that she dreaded that silence.

Most times when she awoke from the dream, she had tears in her eyes. Her heart ached. She'd read a couple of books about baby loss and they said it was normal to feel grief afterwards, but that didn't help. Aunt Joan had tried to get her to get counselling – even just to go and see her local doctor to talk – but Lila hadn't wanted to. She didn't want to talk about it. If she didn't talk about it, she could pretend it never happened. And it was just a miscarriage. It happened all the time. *People didn't talk about these things…*

That was the harsh phrase that Lila disciplined herself with after the dream, as if telling herself off about being so sentimental would stop the dreams coming. *It's not something you talk about.* Yet, if anything, the dreams were coming more frequently.

She got out of bed, pushing the patchwork quilt aside and opening the curtains to look at the rain which was coming down in sheets. The sky was a dark grey. Everything in the garden below dripped; April showers lasted into May in Cornwall, it seemed.

It was still early: she looked at her bedside clock. Seven forty-five on a Sunday morning. So much for a lie-in. She could have stayed home: she could have gone back to bed, but she was up now, and always found it hard to go back to sleep once she was awake. A nagging voice in her mind added *and if you don't go back to sleep, you won't have the dream.* She didn't want the dream. She wished it would go away and leave her alone.

Lila had a quick shower and pulled on a T-shirt and sweater, the jeans she didn't mind getting wet and a pair of black wellington boots. She tied her curly red hair up in a scarf and put on her coat, a thick puffy one with a fur hood. Last, she opened the cupboard, took out a cereal bar and made a quick tea in her insulated travel cup.

The top of Magpie Point was blustery to the point of knocking Lila off her feet, and the rain blew in at her from the side. She'd already got pretty wet walking up through the village and along the coast path, following the headland that was dotted with heather and lavender bushes. Small white flowers sat in clumps low to the ground, and the rain had drenched some late bright yellow daffodils.

It helped, being outside and walking. This was something Lila had never done in London. There were people who loved walking in the city, but she'd never really got into it. Having worked there all week, it felt like too much of an effort to go back in to walk its grimy streets. But here, the sea was a few minutes away at all times. She could hear it from the café on a blustery day. Salt spray was always in the air; Lila breathed deeply, feeling the cold in her lungs. It wasn't bad: it was a kind of cleansing. Walking was her meditation.

Exploring the cliffs around Magpie Cove – all of which overlooked the sandy beach below, to greater or lesser extent – had gradually toned her body. No one talked about the physical aftermath of a miscarriage. She'd been sore and weak for weeks, and it wasn't as though she'd been that fit before then, either. The walking, the view and the air had all helped her. At first, she'd puffed her way up the sharp hills, too, but over time, her legs had got stronger and the aerobic exercise had done her the world of good after everything her body had been through.

And, Lila reflected as she admired the view, if you were going to be around cake every day of your working life, it was probably quite important to stay active.

The small village of Magpie Cove sat between two outcroppings of high, jagged cliffs that plunged dangerously into the Cornish sea. Like many of the places people had chosen to live in around the Cornish coast, the flat sandy cove of the small beach provided a protection of sorts against the harsh weather that could drive in crashing waves, heavy storms and murderously cold seas, particularly in winter.

Lila could well believe in the old tales of smugglers, their boats sunk on the treacherous, sharp rocks that lay hidden under the water. However, standing on top of the cliff and looking out over the sea gave Lila a sense of peace. Whatever the weather, the view of the white-tipped, green-grey sea in winter, or the calm blue seas she'd seen in the late spring, made her feel part of something bigger than herself. Something unchanging, constant and deeply alive.

Lila took a drink of tea from her insulated cup and continued to stare out at the sea that joined the horizon. Blue on blue. It was already pretty warm, though it was always windier up on the cliffs.

She didn't dare go to the edge of the cliff path – the wind was too strong – though she wanted to look down at the churning green-grey sea and lose herself in the vision of the white-tipped waves. Instead, she sheltered by an information board that shook in the wind. She'd read its description of the common wildlife found around Magpie Point, like the sea birds that nested in the cliffs and the unusual green serpentine rock found nearby. Behind the transparent protective pane of all-weather plastic was a faded sticker detailing the local rescue operations. Cornwall was renowned for its harsh weather and changeable, dangerous tides – never mind the hidden submerged rocks in the bays and inlets.

A movement caught her eye on the rock: from where she stood, even though she wasn't at the edge, she could see something in the distance. At first, she thought it was one of the cormorants that sometimes sailed around the black stone cliffs, alighting on the rock face. Peering into the rain, she realised it was a climber.

The person – she couldn't tell if it was a man or a woman – was much further away than she had initially perceived, halfway up or down the rock face, distanced from Magpie Point, more towards where the coastal rock came to a ridge that stretched out into the sea. Lila frowned; the weather was far too wild for anyone to be out climbing. *They must have set out earlier, before the rain,* she thought. *In which case they've been out a long time and must be tired.* It was unusual weather for a May day, certainly. It would be easy to be fooled.

She watched the figure with some concern; she could just make out the fact that they were attached to safety ropes, but if they'd been out climbing for hours, in the cold wind and rain, they would definitely be suffering. She wondered why they hadn't climbed back to the top: perhaps they couldn't.

The climber was at a place on the rock that Lila knew wasn't very accessible; it was a steep drop that she definitely wouldn't risk scrabbling down in her wellingtons. If they were in trouble, she wouldn't be able to get to them in time. Just then, lightning cracked across the sky. As she watched, the climber slipped on their rope and dangled for a moment in the air over the treacherous, roiling sea. Lila didn't think she imagined the cry piercing the air.

Lila ran back to the information board and found the coast-guard number on it. If the climber was fine, then they might be annoyed that she'd called for help, but she knew she'd only worry if she didn't. She tapped the coastguard number into her phone and went back as close to the edge of the cliff as she dared to see where the climber was now. She hadn't yet pressed the call button.

For a moment, Lila's gaze searched the rock. She couldn't see the climber. *Oh no,* she thought. *Was it too late already?* Then she saw them: they had moved temporarily into a kind of crevice in the rock, and were now steadily ascending again. Her finger hovered above the call button. Up and up they went, and after a minute or so they had reached the top of the outcropping. From there, Lila knew it was safe to come up to the main path.

She sipped some tea from her mug and ate the cereal bar, watching the climber and feeling the stress slowly leave her stomach. That had been close. She watched them walk along the top of the rock and disappear onto the other side, then onto the cliff path leading down from the long summit and into a deserted bay. Lila started following, picking up her pace, intending to catch up with the climber and check they were all right. But by the time she got to the ledge from which the climber must have accessed the path, she couldn't see anyone. It was possible that they'd parked a car further down by the bay and driven off already.

Lila was relieved that nothing bad had happened, but she'd wanted to talk to the climber, whoever they were. She wanted to check they were all right, and then, she realised, to give them a piece of her mind. Climbing the rocks around Magpie Point when there was nobody around, so early in the morning, was a stupid thing to do. She didn't care how good a climber they thought they were – if something had happened, she would have been the only person there to possibly prevent it.

Her stomach growled. Maybe it was the tension of the moment. She took in a few deep breaths, feeling like she'd side-stepped a major bit of drama. Her heart was still banging in her chest from the tension; despite the tea and snack, she felt a little light-headed. Just the fact of being on the verge of calling the emergency services brought back that day when the ambulance had arrived.

It felt like a good time to turn around and go home. She'd make a proper breakfast when she got back. The thought was reassuring.

Sometimes, Sundays were lonely. The rest of her week was busy: she had college and her course work, and working in the café – usually, anyway. But on Sundays, often she didn't speak to anyone. It was all right, it was only a day, but on Sundays her thoughts could often stray to losing the baby, of leaving Tim and London, and wondering whether she'd really made the right decision. She knew that she had, deep in her heart, but she worried that she was getting older, and at least with Tim she had had a boyfriend and a chance at marriage, kids: all the normal things. The normal things that she wanted. But she'd wasted years with Tim, and now here she was, a single thirty-something who lived alone and whose main activity was making desserts for other people.

At least I didn't witness anyone perish on the cliffs, though, she told herself. *No need to stress today.*

Maybe it was the tension of the moment when the climber dangled in mid-air, but as she walked back up the cliff path to the information board, Lila realised that she still felt very anxious, though not about the climber. Even so, it was as though the moment of panic had flung open the door to her own enduring worries.

She hadn't even been on a date since coming to Magpie Cove. She was thirty-three. What if she would never be pregnant again? And, as she drank the last of her tea and felt herself buffeted by the wind, the deeper, more frightening thought came again as it sometimes did: what if she couldn't have children at all? She knew many women had miscarriages and went on to have children without any problems, but what if she wasn't one of those women? What if – even if she ever found someone to have a baby with – one miscarriage would follow another, and another?

Lila pulled the toggle on her fur-lined hood so that it gathered in even closer, keeping the wind out of her ears. At that moment, despite the fact that she never usually wanted to talk about it, she wished she had someone to confide in about the baby; someone to listen, at least. She wished she had been brave enough to tell Serafina. Serafina would have listened and understood, because that's what she did for everyone.

But what would she say? How would she explain her feelings? She had been pregnant for a short time, and she hadn't even known it. The loss was still traumatic, both for the experience itself, which was shockingly out of the blue and painful – she hadn't imagined there would be pain, not that she had ever really thought much about it before it actually happened – and the worries it brought with it afterwards.

She tramped on, back toward the village, trying to think her way around her hurt, as if it was a puzzle to be solved, a problem that just needed the right explanation. Perhaps that was why baking appealed to her. Patisserie was so precise, and failure could be explained by technical things: the temperature of an oven, a too-long or too-short baking time, the wrong ingredient at the wrong moment. But what had happened to her couldn't be explained away that easily. Instead, it was a nightmare that wouldn't leave; it was a shadow on her heart, a hitch in her throat, a weight she couldn't leave behind.

Failure. The word nagged at Lila. She knew it was unfair, but she couldn't leave it behind her. *I'm a failure. As a woman. Maybe my body is wrong, somehow. Maybe this is all there is for me.*

Lots of women didn't have children and it didn't make them failures. Lila knew that. In fact, if she ever heard someone else describe a woman as a failure because she had a miscarriage, or couldn't have children, Lila would have leaped to their defence and said all the things that were true and right and logical: that your worth as a woman wasn't measured by your ability to have a baby, or be a mother. And yet, after what had happened, that was exactly how Lila felt. A failure as a woman because she had failed at being a mother. A concept she had always considered ridiculously old-fashioned.

Lila swallowed the tears that wanted to rise up in her throat and strode on, pushing against the wind. She wouldn't let herself break down in a public place, even though there was no one else around. The voice in her mind said, *What would anyone think if they came across you weeping on top of the cliffs while they were out walking their dog? You'd just make them feel uncomfortable, you'd look ridiculous.* It was the same as the voice that told her, *It's just a miscarriage, people have them all the time.* She was only half aware how harsh and unforgiving that voice was, and how cruel it was to talk to herself in that way. She'd always done it. Being kinder would have felt… she searched for the word. Too *permissive.* Too *lenient.* Better to be stoic than self-indulgent. *It's not something we talk about.*

Lila had never questioned where that voice came from and how it had come to talk to her in such a way, but as she walked along, the rain soaking her coat, she started to think about it.

It wasn't her parents' voices: they had been averagely kind, not too heavily disciplinarian. They had both died when she was young, and she'd been sent to boarding school aged twelve. Aunt Joan, her mother's sister, had been her nominated carer, but Lila had hardly seen her after that. She'd stayed at school in the holidays a lot of the time, preferring to read and remain alone. She liked her own company to some extent, but really, she felt out of place around people. She'd never made any especially close friends, though she could be sociable in groups. Being a satellite member of a group wasn't difficult; it was like working at the café. You could talk about inconsequential things, remember people's names, be pleasant. But you didn't have to be you. You didn't have to invest any of your self, because it hurt to do that. Better to feel the distance around you, like the wind, like the sea air on Magpie Point, a safe buffer where you couldn't be touched by the barbs of others' emotions.

She concluded that it was her own voice in her head, not anyone else's. A voice that had grown up with her, that protected her in its own mean-spirited way. If she told herself not to fuss, not to get upset, that things weren't a big deal – if she squirrelled away her powerful feelings, her terrible grief over the death of her parents, her loneliness at school, and now the miscarriage – she could cope. She could manage. She found herself pitying and even disliking others who complained about the things that happened to them. That they didn't have the same strength as she did. The same reserve, the stiff upper lip. *It's not something we talk about.*

But you can't manage, raged a wave of sudden emotion. Lila felt the wave almost like a cough, but it was a cry. A wail that forced itself out of her. She bent over suddenly, hugging her middle, feeling the grief come but unable to stop it. She had no words for it, just a terrible urge to crouch down, to kneel and wail in the mud. *I can't manage. I can't go on feeling like this.*

Instead, she stopped still in the middle of the deserted coast path and let herself cry. If someone came, then she'd have to look stupid. The tears were unstoppable, like someone had released a switch or punched a hole in a reservoir wall. *Please, someone help me,* she screamed inside her own head. *I don't know what to do. I don't know how to feel this. I don't know how to move on.*

But no one came, for which she was both grateful and sad. Finally, the tears eased and she started to walk again, back to Magpie Cove. Perhaps she did need to talk to someone about this. Like the climber, she was alone in a perilous place, buffeted by the elements of her emotions. Perhaps she could climb up to the top of the rock on her own, and perhaps she couldn't, but for the first time she realised that she must try to ask for help.

Chapter Six

'Oh, damn.' Lila peered through the glass at the front of the culinary college oven. 'I'm not sure if it's had enough time.' She stood up and met her friend Oliver's gaze, then leaned over her worktop so that she could see his oven. 'Is yours rising?'

'Think so?' He held both ends of the tea towel he wore around his neck like a scarf and twirled one end. 'Soufflé school has a new star,' he added in a breathy, Marilyn Monroe voice. 'A *rising* star.' He batted his eyelids.

'Oh, for the love of…' Lila rolled her eyes.

'Come on, Lil. The true test is when it comes out, you know that. Whether it deflates or… er, stands erect.'

'I don't know how it's possible to eroticise a soufflé, but I should have known you'd be the one to do it.' Lila grinned.

'Patisserie is sexy.' Oliver shrugged. 'I can't help it if I just *get* it.'

'Hmm.' Lila crouched down again and checked the oven. 'I think I'm giving mine another two minutes. It just isn't coming up as much as I thought it would.'

'*C'est la vie.*' Oliver raised his eyebrow.

Today they were being graded on savoury and sweet soufflé making. Lila had successfully made a cheese soufflé (which Oliver had called *delightfully retro*) and was now frantically crossing her fingers that her raspberry and white chocolate one would turn out okay. She hadn't shaken off her mood from her cliff walk, but at least college was a good distraction. If you had a reason to get up, put your face on and curl your hair in the morning, it made ignoring your feelings that much easier.

On her drive in that day, she'd wondered whether she could perhaps talk to Oliver about the miscarriage. They'd met on the first day of the course and had a jokey friendship based on camp references, patisserie, movies and music, but she wasn't sure if their relationship was the sort that could take a serious conversation like that.

'So, what's happening at the café?' Oliver was already placing his chocolate and black cherry soufflé onto the board on his workstation; the deliciously dark creation showed no signs of collapse. His savoury choice had been parsnip and bacon.

'Three minutes!' shouted their instructor, Jakob, a florid man in chef's whites that stretched over his generous belly.

'Um. Well, I met Serafina's son, Nathan, who owns it now.' Lila looked at her watch and compared it to the clock at the front of the room. There were ten stainless-steel-topped workstations in all. At the start of the year, everyone had been assigned their station, which contained a set of pans and baking implements, a food processor, a professional food mixer and a drawer containing things like baking parchment, ceramic baking beans for pastry and other essentials. There were two industrial fridges at one end of the room.

'And?'

'And he doesn't know whether he's going to keep the café open or not.'

'Why not? I love Serafina's.' Oliver had a flat in St Ives but sometimes came over to Magpie Cove for a walk along the headland – and had always insisted on visiting Serafina. 'I'll miss the old girl,' he tutted. 'You don't laugh at my jokes as much as she did.'

'I'm just not as nice.' Lila grinned. 'But I dunno… he says he doesn't know if it's profitable. I don't know if Serafina really cared about money that much. And, well…' She wondered if she should mention giving the café food to the pensioners in the village.

'And what?'

'Time!' Jakob shouted.

'Agh!' Lila opened her oven door and reached in for the water-filled oven tray that contained the soufflé in its pot. Carefully, she placed it on top of the cast-iron hob and, even more carefully, picked up the soufflé pot and nudged it onto the display board. *Don't sink, don't sink, don't sink*, she muttered to herself as Jakob began his way around the stations, judging and tasting each soufflé. She cast a quick look at Oliver's Black Forest style soufflé, which was still perfect. *Damn.* Hers was okay, but it was definitely showing signs of shrinking any minute now. Lila willed Jakob to get to her as quickly as possible. He was standing at Maddy Murphy's table, eulogising over her lemon and lime.

'Teacher's pet,' Oliver hissed as they waited for Jakob. 'What were you going to say?'

'Never mind.' Lila flapped a tea cloth at him. 'I need to ask your opinion about something. After,' Lila whispered as Jakob approached their stations: fortunately, her raspberry and white chocolate soufflé was still hanging in there.

'If it's whether that cardigan goes with that skirt, the answer is no.' Oliver looked scandalised.

'It's not, but thanks,' she hissed back. Oliver was dressed in his customary black under his white apron, his short blond hair impeccably arranged with styling wax. Lila made sure that she had a full face of make-up on and had put her hair in rollers the night before college partly because she knew Oliver would comment on it otherwise. She also knew that her darling white cardigan with yellow lemons on it went brilliantly with her vintage houndstooth pencil skirt. Oliver was just being catty.

'Miss Bridges!' Jakob gave her a little bow and stuck his spoon into the soufflé on her board. 'And vot do we have here?'

'Raspberry and white chocolate.' Lila gave him a hopeful smile. 'Mmm.'

*

Lila watched as the instructor made one of his weird eating expressions, pursing his lips and opening his eyes wide. '*Güt!*' He beamed at her. 'Ze nice balance of ze sharp raspberry and sweet chocolate. Good height, nice texture. Vell done!'

'Oh, thanks!' Lila felt a weight leave her shoulders – she'd really been worried about this test. At home, her practice soufflés never worked that well.

'Now, Mr Kay.' Jakob moved serenely to Oliver's station. 'Ve vill see if zis soufflé is as good as ze rest!'

'It's a Black Forest theme.' Oliver grinned beatifically at the teacher. 'German – in your honour, Jakob.'

Lila mouthed *really?* at Oliver behind Jakob's back; Oliver ignored her.

'Ah. Of course, though I am Austrian, but no matter.' Jakob laughed merrily. Lila snort-laughed; Oliver glared at her.

Jakob spooned a generous amount of the chocolate and black cherry soufflé into his mouth.

'Mmm!' He made yummy noises. 'Kirsch also, you added?'

'Yes, Jakob,' Oliver replied meekly.

'A triumph!' the instructor crowed. '*Ja,* Mr Kay, I have to say zat I sink you are ze star today! Vell done.' He moved on to the next station.

Oliver, cheeks flushed with pride, pointed to his own chest.

'A triumph. That's what this is, hon,' he whispered.

'So where in Austria is the Black Forest, again?' she whispered back.

'Shut up.' Oliver grinned serenely.

Lila's phone, resting on the workstation next to her, lit up with a text message. It was from Nathan.

Sorry I haven't been in touch – busy. Is tonight okay to come and get the café keys? Text me your address if so. Thanks, Nathan.

'Ooh, who's that?' Oliver grabbed her phone off the workstation and read her text. 'Nathan, eh? Mr Big Boss. Mr Boss Man.'

'More like Hugo Boss Man.' Lila rolled her eyes. 'He probably sleeps in a suit.'

Oliver's eyes widened. 'Like, are we talking Hugo Boss model? Or out-of-shape middle-aged Boss Man? Because I need to visit the café if it's the first one.'

'Give it back, please.' She held out her hand for her phone. 'He's… he's quite attractive, I suppose. I need to give him the café keys back, that's all.'

'I bet you do. Saucy mare.'

'It's not like that.'

'What is it like then? What does he look like?'

'Cyd and Betty think he looks like a young Cat Stevens.'

Oliver tapped on his phone for a minute, found a picture and turned his screen around so she could see. 'Like this? Hot. I could be into that.'

'Kind of like that, but with shorter hair and more of a capitalist vibe.'

Oliver looked at the picture again. 'Mmm. Okay. Yep, I'm going to need to meet him.'

'Well, you might not have a chance if he shuts the café down at the end of the week.' Lila shrugged.

'Then how come my favourite elderly lesbians have already met him?' Oliver stuck a spoon into his own soufflé and put it in his mouth. 'Mmm. Delicious.'

'They came in for breakfast when he summoned me for the meeting the other day. We weren't open, but they looked so frail, I made Nathan let me give them something.'

'I want to end up like them. Lived together their whole lives. Imagine being gay back in the day, though. Stolen kisses in the air raid shelter—'

'What are you on about? They're not that old. Cyd's eighty, which means she was born in 1940. Stolen kisses, as a five-year-old?'

'Well, you know what I mean. Old people can be gay too, you know.' Oliver spooned more of his soufflé into his mouth.

'I know. Anyway, the thing is, I don't think they're doing that well. I was having a meeting in the café with Nathan and Cyd and Betty came by. They said their Meals on Wheels has changed management and what they're getting now is hardly enough to live on. They don't have any money.'

'Poor things.' Oliver had started to clean up his workstation. 'We could take some stuff around. Make them a Victoria sponge, sausage rolls, that kind of thing?'

'That's a nice idea. They'd love to see you as well, I'm sure.' Lila wiped down her own worktop and carefully placed her mostly whole soufflés in a large Tupperware tub to bring home. 'I had a similar idea the other day, actually.'

'What?'

'Well, when I was at the café, I saw we still had quite a lot in the chest freezers at the back. Serafina got a lot in fresh, like the bread for the sandwiches, cakes, that kind of thing. But she kept meat in the freezer, and pastry, pies, garlic bread. You know.'

'Okay.' Oliver sprayed his stainless-steel top with antibacterial cleaner and moved his used mixing bowls and whisks into the sink. 'So?'

'So, theoretically, what if I gave them some of it?'

'Steal from the café? I don't know, Lil. We could get them some groceries ourselves. From the shop.'

'I know. I just thought, with it going to waste… it was just sitting there.'

Oliver leaned on the counter and frowned at Lila. 'Are you telling me you gave them food out of the freezer?'

Lila felt the same guilt that she'd felt in the café wash over her again. She nodded.

'Serafina would have done it.'

'Right. But what if the café does reopen in a week?'

'It might. But it might not.'

'Look, I don't think it's a huge deal, and I might have done the same thing. But you still need to tell Nathan about it tonight when you see him. For your key-swapping date.'

'It's not a date, Oliver.'

'Sure it isn't, doll. But promise me you'll tell him, anyway.'

'Fine. I'll tell him. It was just a spur-of-the-moment thing. Now I feel bad.'

'Well, he'll probably see it the same way, but on the other hand, if I'd just inherited a business, I wouldn't be too chuffed that my employee was stealing from me. Maybe it wasn't the best thing to do if you're anxious to keep your job.'

'No, I suppose not.' Lila felt terrible now.

'Oh, cheer up. Your heart was in the right place.' He winked at her. 'You put your rollers in last night, didn't you?'

'Yes.' Lila touched her hair self-consciously.

'You might want to put them in again for a bit when you get home. Take them out before he comes round, obviously.'

'Thanks for the tip,' she replied drily.

'Us girls gotta stick together,' Oliver trilled. 'Even when one of us is a *triumph* and the other one isn't. Not my words.'

'Oh, shut up, Oliver.' Lila laughed. She still wasn't sure if she could trust Oliver with her secret, but he was a good friend nonetheless, and she'd never really had that many friends apart from Alice, and she was far away in London. It was a comfort to have someone that made her laugh, and she was thankful for Oliver, for his catty quips – and for the sheer joy of doing what she loved. Yes, there were still dark days, but Magpie Cove filled them with more light than she'd ever known, and she was grateful.

Chapter Seven

At precisely six thirty, as arranged, there was a knock on the door. Lila checked her hair and make-up in the hallway mirror before opening it – there was no point in looking like she'd just got up. Oliver had reminded her that if Nathan was on the fence about reopening the café, then a well-turned-out employee versus a scruffy cow – his words – could possibly swing it either way. Lila doubted that Nathan, from what she'd seen of him so far, was someone who made important business decisions based on someone's outfit, but then he was always very smartly dressed himself. She'd concluded that it didn't hurt to look nice.

'Hi. Come in.' Lila smiled, though her heart was hammering. She'd managed to work herself into a tizzy, worrying about the stolen food. Even though it was in a good cause, she knew she shouldn't have done it. She could have just gone to the supermarket and bought Cyd and Betty some bits and bobs. It was just the thought that all that perfectly good food might go to waste that had done it. And the fact that Cyd had felt so thin when she'd hugged her.

Nathan, dressed impeccably in a pinstripe suit, stood on the doorstep with an odd expression on his face. *Pinstripe? In Magpie Cove?* Lila thought the last time the village had probably seen pinstripe was the 1940s, unless it was on one of the visiting artists who sometimes wore suit jackets over their faded T-shirts and jeans.

'Oh. Thanks.' He seemed curious about the flat, looking at the faded wallpaper and down the hallway into the kitchen. 'Been here long?'

'In the flat? About eight months.'

'How is it, living in the village?'

Lila showed him into the cosy living room.

'Nice.' She shrugged. 'Take a seat. Tea?'

'Tea would be great, thanks.'

'Are you looking for a place? I mean, if you reopen the café – and if you wanted to stay in Magpie Cove – I would have thought your mum's flat would have been the ideal place to stay.' Serafina had lived above the café. It was actually a very nice, large flat: Lila had dreamed about having something as spacious and light. It also had a great view of the sea from the biggest bedroom.

'No, I'm not… just curious, that's all.' He changed the subject. 'Nice fireplace.' The living room was a good size for a one-bedroom flat, high-ceilinged with the original cornicing and a lovely rose at the centre. There was also a Victorian tiled fireplace – which still worked, though the chimney hadn't been swept for a few months.

'Yes. I love period detail.' Lila went to put the kettle on, and was surprised that Nathan followed her.

'Good sized kitchen,' he remarked. 'Perfect for baking.'

'It is.' She got two mugs out of the cupboard, wondering when this odd assessment of the flat would end and they could talk about the café. It was like having tea with an estate agent. Plus, her conscience was shouting at her to come clean.

'Course going well?'

'I think so. I was there today. Soufflés.'

'Did they stay risen? I hear that's the important thing.'

'Fortunately, yes.' Lila opened a tin and took out some oatmeal raisin cookies she'd made a few days earlier, putting them on a plate. 'So – keys. Here you go.' The keys were already on the table. She set the cookies and mugs on the kitchen table which overlooked a row of small back gardens.

'Thanks.' He sat down at the kitchen table and bit into one of the cookies. 'This is amazing,' he said, between chews. 'Really buttery.'

'I made them.' She curtseyed.

'Right… the café.' Nathan took a sip of tea and put the cup back on the table. 'Thanks for your patience on this. I know it's not ideal, not knowing if you've got a job or not.'

'It's not great,' Lila agreed, sipping her tea. She felt a knot of nerves in her stomach. 'Look, I need to tell you something—'

'Why don't I give you the information first, and then you can put your case forward.' Nathan hadn't phrased it as a question.

'Fine.' She'd tell him in a minute. Her stomach felt tight. She hated being dishonest.

'Okay. I've looked at the books, and while the numbers aren't great, I think that may partly be due to Mum's appalling record-keeping. I've talked to people in the village, and you, of course. I know how important the café is to Magpie Cove, and how many people seem to love it. So, I'm going to keep it open for two months and see how it performs, and make a number of improvements. If it's doing well after that time, we'll stay open for a year and then review again,' he continued.

'A month? That still doesn't give me a lot of security.' Lila turned the large amber ring on her finger anxiously.

'I know, but it's the best I can do. I can't guarantee to keep the café open just so you have a job,' he replied, tersely. 'I thought you'd be pleased.'

'I am pleased. I suppose I was just looking for more time than that. While I finish my course. But you're the boss.' She had four months left on the course, more or less. It would be a pain to have to find a new job so close to the end of it, but she couldn't make ends meet without one.

'I am.' He smiled thinly. 'So, you'll come back?'

'Yes. But I need to tell you something first.'

'What is it?' He sat back, arms crossed over his chest. His tone was impatient, like he was talking to a child. It annoyed her, but she was still determined to tell him.

'The other day, when we were in the café? After you left, I gave a bit of the food from the freezer to Cyd and Betty. For free. I'm sorry, I shouldn't have done it, but they're really frail and they were telling me about how Meals on Wheels has got really rubbish recently and I felt awful having all that food there in the freezer, just going to waste if the café didn't reopen. I'll pay for it, whatever it cost… I just wanted to tell you. I've never done anything like that before.'

Nathan gazed at her for a long moment, not saying anything. A smile briefly played around his lips, but then he cleared his throat and his serious expression returned.

'Is that it?' he asked her, flatly.

'Yes. I'm sorry. Again. I will pay for it.'

'And what was it that you took? Exactly?' His arms remained crossed, but she couldn't read his expression. She listed the items faithfully.

He gave her a long look.

'You seem quite worried,' he observed.

'Of course I am. I feel terrible about it, actually. Although I do honestly think your mum would have done the same thing. That's what made me do it, if I'm honest,' Lila gabbled. She tried to take a deep breath and calm down.

He regarded her silently for a minute.

'Fine. Well, I appreciate you letting me know, but to be quite honest, I think we can manage without some sausages and a few garlic baguettes. I mean, I'm not telling you to continue giving our stock away, now that we're reopening, but I appreciate that I was unfairly vague with you in that meeting, so you had good reason to believe you were redistributing food that otherwise might have gone to waste.'

Lila felt all the tension in her stomach melt away. She couldn't believe what she was hearing.

'Oh my goodness. Are you sure?'

'Lila, it's just a few frozen sausages. As I said, I appreciate the honesty, but let's move on, okay? In the grand scheme of things, it's nothing.'

'Right… okay.' Whatever she'd expected, it wasn't this. It had been a stupid mistake and she wouldn't be doing it again, but somehow she thought a humourless businessman like Nathan would have hit the roof. *It just shows that you can't ever make assumptions about people*, she thought. 'So when are we reopening?'

'Next week, I thought, if that suits you?' He tapped at his phone.

'Okay. I'll give you my schedule. The days I usually work.' She went to the kitchen counter to get a piece of paper and a pen.

'Mum was there on her own when you weren't there?' He looked down at his notebook. 'I forgot you were part time.'

'Yes. I work all day Saturday, and every day in the week apart from Tuesday and Friday which are my college days. Serafina closed on Sundays and she covered Tuesday and Friday. She was usually around on the days I was there, on and off. So you'll need someone for those other days,' she prompted him.

'Right. Any ideas? They need to be able to start next week.' He frowned.

'I'll think about if I know anyone. But it's really not that hard. You could do it.' Lila sipped her tea, watching him over the rim of the mug. His face looked like she'd just asked him to muck out a pigpen.

'Me? Work in a café?'

'Why not? It's mostly making sandwiches and drinks and bringing them to people. I can help you plan the menu, show you how the coffee machine works, that kind of thing.' She tried not to laugh at his horrified expression. 'Unless you've got somewhere else you need to be? I mean, I don't mean to pry, but I know you work in London. If you're just going to be here a couple of days, then obviously you can't do it. I just… it would be good to know if you're going to be around. For the café?'

That shadow crossed his face again, like she'd seen at the funeral: he had a way of suddenly cutting off, or smoothing all emotion from his features.

'I'll be around. I… I don't need to be back in London for a while.' His tone didn't sound like he wanted her to ask any more questions, but Lila pressed on. It was fair to want to know if her new boss was going to disappear at a moment's notice.

'You're moving here permanently?'

'No. But I'm here for now.' He stood up. 'I'd better be going.'

'You don't have to go.' Lila stood up and touched him on the arm. 'I'm sorry. It's none of my business. You need to stay because we need to talk about the food stock. If you want to reopen the café in a week.'

Lila's phone rang: it was an unfamiliar number.

'Excuse me,' she said. 'I don't often get calls from numbers I don't know. I'm just going to get this, just in case…' She had a strange feeling that she had to pick up the call. She couldn't explain it, but it was as though someone was standing next to her, telling her to answer it.

'Go ahead.' Nathan turned to the window and looked out, moodily.

'Hello?' Lila answered the call.

'Lila Bridges?' She didn't recognise the woman's voice at the other end of the call.

'Yes?' Her heart started beating fast. Something was wrong.

'Hello. This is Laura Anderson from St Ives General Hospital. I'm a nurse there.'

'Oh my …. Is it… is everything all right? Who…' Lila trailed off.

'We have a patient here – Cyd Bassett? Her friend Betty asked me to call you.'

'Cyd? Is she okay?' Lila sat down on the kitchen chair, her heart racing.

'She's had a bad fall and broken her leg,' the nurse explained. 'She hit her head when she fell as well. She's okay, and Betty was with her when they brought her in. Betty asked that I call you so you could bring some of their things to hospital, as Cyd's going to need to stay for a little while. Betty said you'd know where the key was?'

'Oh. Yes, I do. That's fine, of course, I'll come right away.' Lila caught Nathan's eye; he looked concerned.

'Thank you. Betty would have rung herself, but she didn't want to leave Cyd.'

'All right.'

The nurse listed a few things Cyd wanted. 'Ward C, when you get here. It's easy to find.'

'Okay. Thanks for letting me know.' Lila pressed the red circle to end the call. She stared in shock at the phone.

'What was that about? Are you all right?' Nathan looked uncomfortable, like he wasn't sure what to do. 'You've gone white.'

'I'm okay. It's Cyd. One of the old ladies that were at the café the other day.'

'Oh, right. Is she okay?'

'She's had a fall. Broken her leg.' Lila's voice wavered and she started to cry. 'I'm sorry. It's… I'm just a bit upset. I've been really worried about Cyd and Betty and now… this has happened.'

'Of course.' Nathan gathered her into his arms and gave her a hug. His former cold manner had evaporated. Lila was surprised, but it felt good to be comforted.

'I've got to go. I said I'd get some of Cyd's things and bring them to the hospital. I'm sorry, but can we… finish talking later?' Lila wiped her eyes and looked around for her car keys. Once, when she'd walked Cyd and Betty back to their house, carrying their shopping, Betty had shown her a spare key under a flowerpot. *Just in case, maid,* she'd said at the time. Well, now was the *just in case* moment.

'I'll drive you, it's fine. My car's just outside.' Nathan got up.

'You don't need to do that. I'll be okay.'

'Don't be silly. I'm happy to. And those hospital car parks are a bloody nightmare to find a space in anyway. If I drive you, you can hop out when we get there and I'll find you when I've parked. Okay?'

'Oh, well, if you're sure. Thanks.' Lila looked around for a jacket, found the black patent Mary Janes she'd worn to college that day and slipped them on. 'Right. Let's go. I'll direct you to their house. It's a few streets away.'

They walked out of the flat and down the steps that led to the street. Lila locked the door behind her and followed Nathan to a shiny black BMW parked nearby. He pointed the key at it and its lights flashed.

'This is yours?' Lila slid into the passenger seat, feeling suddenly grateful that he couldn't see her ancient green VW Beetle. 'Very swish.'

'Oh, it's just a rental,' he said dismissively. Lila guessed that new, top-of-the-range cars weren't a big deal to Nathan DaCosta. They were to most people in Magpie Cove, though.

The car purred to life and Lila pointed to the end of the street.

'That way and then right, then left,' she said. He drove carefully up the twisty streets. 'Follow this along for a bit and then there's a little lane to the right. That's where the house is, but park at the end of the lane. You'll never get the car out if you drive it up there,' she instructed. Nathan pulled in where she indicated, making a face as a local driver zoomed past him with hardly any room to spare.

'These roads are a nightmare,' he muttered.

'I won't be long.' Lila hopped out and walked up to Cyd and Betty's house. She nudged the big flowerpot with her knee and found the key underneath. Shaking her head, she let herself into the tiny cottage. Only somewhere like Magpie Cove could you confidently leave a key under a pot and not expect someone to break in.

Inside, the house was neat and tidy but very obviously belonged to two elderly ladies. In the cosy lounge, books, newspapers and magazines were piled up next to two aged adjustable brown easy chairs, both of which had a table-on-wheels next to it. A walking frame stood in the corner, with a cardigan draped over it. Lila wondered whether to take a couple of books in for Cyd: she picked up a romance and a biography of Queen Elizabeth I.

The cottage was in fact a large bungalow, with the bedroom at the back. Lila felt odd going into Cyd and Betty's private space, but Betty had asked her to bring a few changes of clothes for them both, so she had to do it. She unfolded a large tote bag she'd brought with her from home and opened some drawers, putting a few sets of cardigans, skirts and underclothes into it. Everything in the drawers was neatly pressed, and the mustard and brown 70s-style bedcover was smoothed perfectly over the sheets on the bed. Cyd and Betty might have found it difficult to get around, but they were evidently still house proud.

Lila went into the kitchen next, more out of curiosity than anything. She opened some of the old-fashioned blue formica cabinets: inside one there were a few cans of beans, and in another some chicken noodle soup packets. In the fridge was some cheese, a bit of butter and what looked like two uneaten Meals on Wheels dinners. Lila peeked through the transparent lid: each seemed to contain a slice of cheap-looking ham, some cold cooked carrots and one boiled potato.

She shook her head. Elderly people deserved better. They needed more: their health would suffer if they didn't eat well.

Locking the front door behind her, Lila tucked the key carefully back under the flowerpot outside and carried the tote bag back to Nathan's car.

'Let's go.' She put the bag in the back and slid back into the front seat. 'I'll give you directions.'

'No need.' Nathan frowned. 'I remember the way.'

Chapter Eight

'Nathan's keeping the café open. I've been back in this week.' Lila opened a Tupperware box containing sandwiches she'd made at home, and another containing a batch of madeleines she'd made especially for Cyd and Betty. 'Here.' She placed them on the little table next to Cyd's bed. It was Lila's third visit to the elderly couple, and this time she'd brought Oliver with her. That first night when Nathan had driven her, she hadn't been able to talk to Cyd, who was asleep. Betty had told her what had happened: Cyd had slipped on the kitchen floor. It was such an easy thing to do when you were frail, and Lila feared it would become more and more likely. She'd had a text from Alice on her way to the hospital, asking how she was doing – she'd answer it later. She was aware that she often forgot to reply to Alice at all or answered days late. It was only her friend checking in, but Lila's instinct was not to talk about her life if she could avoid it, even by text.

'Oh, well that's a relief, my love!' Betty reached for a madeleine and handed one to Cyd. 'Here, Cyd. Your favourite.'

'Ooh, I loves a madeleine. Thank you, Lilly.' Cyd broke a piece off the soft, buttery cake and ate it carefully. 'Food in here's not much to write 'ome about, I must say.' Lila had stopped correcting Cyd and Betty calling her Lilly a long time ago. They always forgot, anyway.

'I brought you something too.' Oliver leaned over and kissed Cyd's papery cheek.

'Oh, he's a good boy. So nice to see you too, my love.' Cyd's face lit up. She adored Oliver. 'What've you made me, you naughty boy? Somethin' very bad for me, I 'ope.'

'Red velvet cupcakes.' Oliver opened his Harrods cake tin and showed them both the swirls of cream cheese frosting atop eight cherry red cakes.

Nathan had stayed with her that first visit, patting her back slightly awkwardly as she'd watched poor Cyd asleep in the hospital bed, Betty dozing in the chair next to her. He'd bought her a cup of tea in the café and they'd sat there, not really saying anything, before they went up and checked on Cyd again. The nurses had assumed that Nathan was Lila's husband, and she hadn't had the energy to correct them. He'd driven her home, dropping her at her front door. When she'd thanked him, he'd brushed it off. *Don't be silly. I wouldn't let you go in on your own. Hospitals are awful places,* he'd said as she got out of his sleek car.

For a brief moment then, she'd wondered whether to tell him about losing the baby. It was ridiculous, she hardly knew him, but she'd wanted to – just for a brief moment. They'd become something else in the hospital – temporarily, he'd changed from a remote work acquaintance to someone who comforted her, joked gently with her about the crappy tea in the hospital cafeteria, who had driven home silently as she'd nodded off in the passenger seat.

Of course, she hadn't said anything. Hadn't told him that she'd been in a hospital too, all too recently. That she hated its smell. Hated the noise and the constant hustle and bustle. *It's not something we talk about,* she'd reminded herself. *And certainly not to people we hardly know.*

'Enough cakes for the whole ward here!' Betty laughed. 'Oh, don't worry, Cyd. I won't give them away before you've stuffed yourself, I'm sure. Look at 'er face.'

It was true that Cyd did look mortified at the idea of sharing her cakes. There were ten beds, five on one side and five facing them, and all of their inhabitants were elderly women.

'So, listen, Cyd. How's the leg?' Lila asked.

'Well, I did break it.' Cyd sighed. 'So, what with me bein' an old fart an' all, I've probably got to be here a good few weeks while it heals up enough for me to go home. Bloody rubbish if you ask me, but there 'tis.'

'Cyd's bones are brittle these days,' Betty explained. 'Osteoporosis. Snaps like a twig if she so much as sneezes.'

'No more lindy-hopping for us.' Cyd took Betty's hand. 'We were ballroom champions too once, years ago. Have I told you that? 'Course, in the competitions, they usually didn't let us dance together. We had a couple of fellas that were an item who danced too, so we used to couple up with them. Peter and David. Lovely boys they were. You remind us of them a bit, duck.' She patted Oliver's hand.

'Were they devilishly handsome?' Oliver ran a hand through his perfectly styled blond hair.

'Oh, very nice. Both passed away now, mind you.' Cyd looked wistful.

'You weren't allowed to dance girl-girl? In the competitions?' Oliver asked, taking a madeleine from the box.

'Oh, no. Times was different then, my love. Not like now.' Betty bit into one of the sandwiches.

'Wasn't there a lesbian dance league of some kind?' Oliver asked.

'What, in Cornwall, in the 70s? Lord have mercy.' Betty clicked her tongue. 'Wasn't like we lived in London. We always had to keep that side of things quiet. We didn't mind, most of the time. But I would have loved to dance with Cyd at a championship.' Betty looked mistily at Cyd, lying in the bed. 'I'm sorry, Lilly, if we've shocked you. You might not have known about us being…' she looked around her and mock-whispered in a dramatic voice, '… *lesbians*.'

'Um… I knew.' Lila tried not to giggle.

'Oh, we're not ashamed, my love,' Cyd interrupted. 'But I know we'd never really mentioned it before. In the café and suchlike. Old 'abits. Time was, people could take offence. Peter and David got set upon more than once, just for 'olding 'ands.'

Lila felt terrible: had she created an environment where Cyd and Betty had felt they couldn't be themselves? She didn't think so – Magpie Cove had always felt like a friendly place where everyone was welcome. But then, it was easy for her to say that – she wasn't an elderly lesbian.

'Speaking of the café,' Oliver interjected. 'Tell Cyd and Betty all about Nathan's terrible schemes.'

'Oh, goodness.' Lila covered her face with her hands. 'I don't know where to start.'

It had been great to reopen the café and start to get back to normal, but on their second day, Nathan had begun a series of *initiatives* aimed at making the café more profitable. It was like there were two Nathans: the thoughtful one that had been there for her when she had looked through the glass partition at Cyd, small and vulnerable in her hospital bed, and the cold, money-obsessed one that was systematically stripping the café of all its charm.

'Initiatives?' Betty looked blank. 'Whassat mean?'

'Well, you know. Ways to make more money,' Lila explained. She felt oddly unfaithful to the nice Nathan by talking about his terrible plans for the café – he had been so kind to her at the hospital, before.

'Like what?' Cyd asked.

'Well, he's put the prices of the food up, for one thing. Everything's gone up twenty per cent.'

'Even our breakfasts? I s'pose Serafina never put the prices up since the Berlin Wall come down.' Cyd chortled. 'I am lookin' forward to my sausage 'n' egg 'n' beans, mind you, when I get back.'

'Well, I persuaded him to keep the breakfasts more or less as they were. Ten per cent rather than twenty.' Lila shrugged. 'I explained how it's only really you two, Rovina and Eric and a couple of others that ever make it in for the early bird special.'

'Well, that's not too bad, my love.' Betty shrugged. 'We can cope with that.'

'Oh, I'm just getting started.' Lila shook her head. 'He doesn't want people to stay too long in the café. People who get a coffee and a cake and work on their laptops for the morning – he doesn't like that. He's imposing a £5 per person charge for stays longer than an hour if they're not buying lunch or dinner. It's really unfriendly. Part of why people love Serafina's is that there was no pressure, it felt like home. People might only have paid for a coffee and a cake but most came every day.' Lila crossed her arms. 'He also thinks we pay too much for bread and cakes – we get them from Maude in the bakery opposite. People love that bread. Maude already does us a great deal, but he's not happy. We're getting things like bread and cakes in from a wholesaler now. The quality's terrible compared to what we had.'

'Maude can't be happy about losing the business either.' Oliver pursed his lips. 'Such a shame.'

'I know. I've tried to explain to him that the café is a hub for the community. But he won't see it. I dunno. I guess he lived here when he was young, but then he went away to London and hardly ever came back. He just doesn't get it.'

'I'm all for modernisation, duck, but it don't sound like he really understands Magpie Cove. People're loyal to Serafina. They loved 'er. We loved 'er.' Betty raised an eyebrow. 'I'm not so sure that her Nathan's goin' to be loved quite as much.'

'I don't think so either. People are already complaining.' Lila bit into a red velvet cupcake gloomily. 'Ugh. I should have guessed this would be more delicious than my madeleines.'

'Of course it is,' Oliver tutted. 'Star pupil, aren't I? Look, all you need to do is hang on at the café until you graduate at the end of the year, and then the world's your oyster. You won't need a little café in Magpie Cove. You'll be sailing the coves of the world in a private yacht, making patisserie for an eligible billionaire.'

'Hmm. That's your dream, not mine, Oliver.' Lila wiped the perfect cream cheese frosting from her lips. 'Nathan's talked about setting up a private catering company. I want to see where that goes. And… I don't know. I like Magpie Cove. I'm not ready to leave just yet.'

'You stay where you are, my love.' Betty patted Lila's hand. 'I'm a little bit psychic, y'know, an' I reckon somethin' good's comin' your way. Maybe even a nice-lookin' young man.' She winked and started humming 'Morning Has Broken'.

'Ooh, that Cat Stevens had a lovely voice,' Cyd said, picking up another madeleine and taking a bite.

'You two are terrible,' Lila laughed. It was such a relief to see Cyd coming back to her normal self. Betty hadn't left her side, either – the nurses had set up a bed for her next to Cyd in the ward. Lila thought of what Oliver had said about how amazing it must have been to have loved the same person for a lifetime. It seemed so out of her grasp right now – but it was good to know it was possible.

Chapter Nine

'Pretty quiet for a Friday.' Oliver sat down on one the stools at the café counter and looked around him.

'I know. Usually I'd be run off my feet. Cappuccino?'

'Large please. Ta.'

Lila selected one of the large blue wash pottery cups and saucers from the cupboard under the counter and turned her back to Oliver to start the milk foamer. She'd been feeling a little better: she hadn't had a nightmare for a while, and had been so run off her feet with college work that she hadn't had time to think about anything other than pastry. She knew that she was doing what she always did: ignore the problem, lock it away. But concentrating on her course did help her manage her feelings, even if it wasn't healthy in the long run.

'Nathan around?' Oliver whispered.

'No. He's due back soon, though.' Lila ground the coffee beans and set the cup under the coffee spout of the machine. 'Other fish to fry. Metaphorically, that is. I don't think he's ever cooked anything in his life.'

'Hm. So how's it going with his new initiatives, then?' Oliver picked up the menu and perused it. 'I assume the sandwiches aren't worth it anymore?'

'Not really. Lasagne's still good at lunch. The muffins aren't bad.'

'I'll take a punt on a muffin, then.'

Lila selected one of the bran and raisin muffins from under the glass dome, put it on a matching plate and set it on the counter in front of Oliver.

'We used to take all our cakes from Maude too. She's being nice about us cancelling the order but it's so awkward.' Lila made a face. 'Obviously, it was me that had to go and tell her: he wouldn't get his own hands dirty. Our order makes up a lot of Maude's turnover, I think. I feel terrible about it.'

It had indeed not been pleasant to break the news to Maude, and ever since, things had felt a little strained between them. Lila had done her best to be friendly about it – and she'd been into the bakery opposite to buy herself lunch and various cakes and treats far more than she would have done usually, to try to make up for it. Still, she didn't blame Maude for being put out. Maybe Maude thought that Lila had chosen Nathan over her: it was like school, where the girls in Lila's class or in her dorm room would switch alliances at the drop of a hat. Lila would lose count of the times that she was suddenly cold-shouldered out of one friend group or adopted into another. Being a grown-up shouldn't be like that: it *wasn't* like that, not really. Only, this made it feel that way, and it bothered Lila, because it broke the harmony of living in Magpie Cove.

Oliver bit into the muffin. 'Hm. Average at best. Poor Maude.'

'I know.' Lila looked around at the empty café. 'You can see how quiet it gets now – it was never like this before. People really don't like this maximum stay rule. And I hate having to keep explaining it. It's not Nathan who has to take the flak. He comes in for a few hours most days, but he sits in the corner at his laptop most of the time unless I make him help out.'

'What about when you're not working?'

'He's recruiting for someone to cover the rest of the hours. Haven't had many applicants, though.'

'Just remember: stick it out to the end of the course, then it's private yacht time.' Oliver picked a raisin out of the muffin and inspected it.

'Right.' Lila grinned. 'So what brings you this way? I didn't know you were visiting.'

'I wanted to chat to you about Cyd and Betty.' Oliver sipped his coffee. 'I'm worried about them.'

'I know. I mean, I'm glad Cyd's okay, but they're getting more and more frail. And I'm really concerned about their food. I saw what they had in their house, Oli. Almost nothing. I was thinking, maybe we could… I dunno. Do something. They're not the only elderly people that are half starving to death.'

'We could bring them food. Sort of on a rota, between us?' Oliver suggested.

'We could. But I was thinking about something a bit nicer.' Lila leaned on the counter.

'What?'

'Well, Meals on Wheels is terrible, right? Apparently, they've changed their provider or something and whoever's running it at the moment is hardly giving the oldies enough to live on. And it's not exactly delicious.'

'Right. So?'

'So, what if we could raise enough money to kind of take over feeding the elderly in Magpie Cove? For a year at least, or a few months. Supplement what they have. It would just be an extra service.'

Oliver drank his coffee and replaced the mug on its blue saucer.

'It's a massive undertaking. We'd have to be cooking every day and then distributing all the food. It's a full-time job, Lila, and we've got our finals coming up, you've got your job here… I think it sounds brilliant, but I don't think we can do it. Not like that anyway.'

Lila nodded.

'You're right. I dunno, I just get really upset when I think about Cyd and Betty having to rely on a few carrots and a bit of cheese.'

'Well, the idea is good. What's a more do-able version of the idea? Something once a week, maybe?'

'Like a weekly cake delivery?' Lila wondered aloud. 'I mean, it's nothing like the same thing. You can't live on cake.'

'Well, you could, in theory, but what about a weekly delivery and it's cake and bread and maybe a few other bits. We might be able to get donations. Maude might help us out with bread. We can make the cakes. It's something, isn't it? At least it's a bit of cheer once a week.'

'How many people are we talking about, do you think?' Lila wondered. 'There must be a way to find out. There's probably a lot of people too fragile to leave the house who we don't know about.'

'You probably can't ring up the council and ask. Data protection and all that. The locals would be the best bet. Cyd and Betty might know?'

'They've certainly lived here a long time.' Lila looked up as the bells strung to the door jangled and Nathan strode in. 'Uh-oh. Let's talk about this later, okay?'

'Many people been in?' Nathan dropped his briefcase behind the counter and took off his smart coat. Underneath, he wore a dark blue suit with a white shirt open at the neck. He ran a hand through his black curly hair which looked as though it was starting to grow out. Lila felt a pleasant tremor somewhere in the region of her belly and was immediately mortified. Yes, Nathan DaCosta was technically attractive – and when he'd hugged her that night at her flat, it had felt… right, somehow. But he was ruining the café, he was brusque and tactless and only cared about money.

However, Lila could also see that Oliver was dying to be introduced.

'Nathan, this is a friend of mine, Oliver Kay. Oli, this is Nathan DaCosta. Serafina's son,' she added, as if she and Oli hadn't been gossiping about Nathan for weeks already.

'I know what you're thinking – *O-Kay*. My parents' little joke, though they deny it.' Oliver shook Nathan's hand. 'In fact, I'm nothing less than sensational.'

Lila snorted with laughter, but Nathan shook Oliver's hand solemnly.

'Nice to meet you,' he said, seriously, and glanced around the café. 'Bit quiet today?' He looked searchingly at Lila.

'It is,' she replied. She wasn't going to lie. 'People aren't keen on some of your new initiatives. There have been a few complaints.'

As if to demonstrate her point, the door opened again and a couple of surfers came into the café: Lila could tell because they had their dry wetsuits on under hoodies and surf shoes on. They sat down at a table and Lila took a deep breath: she picked up a couple of menus and took them over.

'Hi, welcome to Serafina's.' She smiled warmly at the man and woman. 'Have you visited before?'

'No. We're going to surf at the cove a bit later, but we heard the café here was great – can we get a couple of coffees?' the woman asked.

Lila dreaded giving them the spiel, but she knew she had to, especially with Nathan watching.

'Sure. Just to let you know, we're now operating an hour maximum rule for anyone not ordering a full meal,' she explained.

'Sorry?' The man gave her a funny look. Lila's stomach clenched. She hated this. It was so counter-intuitive. If you wanted people to come back to the café, surely it made more sense to make them as happy and comfortable as possible?

'Er, yes. Sorry about that. I'll get your coffees, though.'

The couple exchanged looks.

'Can't say that's what I expected,' the woman said. 'Serafina's is supposed to be this amazing, one-of-a-kind cosy hangout. Surfers from all around talk about it. No one mentioned the time limit.'

'No. Well, it's a very new development,' Lila said in a low voice, still smiling. 'I'm afraid Serafina herself passed away recently.'

'That's a shame. I was looking forward to meeting her,' the woman continued. 'A friend of ours was telling us, once he was here surfing for the weekend and she did an impromptu lockdown. Cocktails all night, they had a limbo competition, the works. *Legendary.*'

Lila's stomach turned again as she realised how quickly everything Serafina had worked for was going to disappear if Nathan continued with his changes.

'That sounds like Serafina,' she said sadly. 'She was one of a kind.'

'New management, is it?' the man asked in a low voice, looking at Nathan and Oliver at the counter.

'Umm... yes.' Lila didn't want to be disloyal – or for Nathan to overhear the conversation. 'Let me get those drinks for you, anyway.'

She returned to the counter and started the coffee machine again. There was an awkward silence. Oliver gave her a look; she'd thought that he and Nathan had been chatting at the counter, but Nathan seemed to be immersed in some paperwork.

'All okay over there?' Oliver asked pointedly.

'Oh. Fine.' Lila glared at him. It would be just like Oliver to cause trouble out of sheer nosiness.

'Hmm.' Oliver raised his eyebrow. 'Well, I'm going to leave you to it. Wouldn't want to outstay my welcome.' He looked pointedly at his watch.

'I'll catch up with you later, Oli.' Lila gave him a fixed smile that meant *stop it.* She needed this job, for a little longer at least.

'I'm going, I'm going.' Oliver sashayed out of the café, throwing her a meaningful look as he did so. She knew she'd hear exactly what Oliver thought about Nathan the next time she was at college: Oliver would spare no detail.

'So he's your…?' Nathan left the sentence hanging.

'Friend?' Lila put Oliver's cup and plate in the dishwasher. 'He's on my patisserie course.'

'Oh. Well, if he wants some work, I need another pair of hands for this afternoon tea we've got booked.' Nathan didn't seem perturbed by Oliver's flirting with him, and Lila wondered for a moment whether he had thought she and Oliver were an item. It seemed a ridiculous notion to her, but she supposed not everyone picked up on Oliver's camp manners at first. Anyway, it wasn't like you had to be gay just because you were camp.

'I'm sure he'd love to. I'll ask.' There was a silence as Lila stacked the dishwasher. 'Coffee?' she stood up and looked at her list of tasks; there wasn't much to do now ahead of lunch.

'Flat white. Please.'

Lila started the process she'd done for Oliver just earlier: the machine that ground the beans and made a thick, strong espresso in a small cup. For a flat white, she repeated the process – a double shot – and poured it into a smaller cup, finishing with a small amount of steamed milk.

'I miss your mum, you know.' She put one of the blue pottery saucers under the cup and slid it across the counter for Nathan. 'This was one of the first things she taught me to do. Use the coffee machine.'

He took the cup and sipped from it.

'I miss her too,' he replied, a little shortly, but not in an unfriendly way. 'I hadn't seen much of her the past few years. No reason, really. I just got kind of tied up with my work and that whole London life, you know. Keeping up with friends. Wine club. Golf club. Dinner parties. Skiing. I should have made more time to come and visit.'

'Well, I don't think that's London for everyone,' Lila replied diplomatically. 'Mine was more office, pub, office, pizza, TV, office…'

'Oh. Well, that's how it was with my friends. The circles I was in.' He picked up his coffee. 'Not that I've heard from them since I've been here.'

'Maybe they're not that good friends, then.'

'Maybe not.' Nathan stared around the café. 'You know, Mum didn't always have the café. She started it after she got divorced. Her parents left her some money – my grandparents weren't short of cash – and she bought this place. It was an ironmonger's or something before, I think. James and I got sent off to school not long after. She thought it was the best thing for us. But when I'd come home in the holidays, she always held a party for us and invited all the locals. There was always a massive cake someone had baked, she'd push all the tables back so everyone could dance. That first half term we came back, she'd changed so much. The café saved her, in a way. She went from a bit of an outsider to the centre of the community.'

'Everyone loved her, that's for sure,' Lila agreed, making a cappuccino for herself. 'Why did she send you away, though?'

'I don't know. I think she didn't want me and James to see her grieve. She wanted the best for us and now she had this money from her parents – when she was married to my dad, they all but ignored us, because they hated the fact he was a Jamaican mechanic. They wanted her to marry someone rich. But when they split up, I guess they wanted to be involved again. I never really knew them much, though, because of being away at school by the time they decided to be grandparents again. She said to us, *what jobs are there for you here*? But I dunno… people live here. It's not impossible.'

'Maybe not for you, though. Maybe she saw that?' Lila suggested. She thought about her own experience of boarding school: for her, it had been different. It was less a choice for brighter career prospects and more somewhere to put her after both her parents died. Aunt Joan said it gave her structure, which she supposed it did. But, Lila thought, if she'd had the choice of a cosy home with someone like Serafina, she would have taken that instead.

'Maybe.' He set his coffee down next to his laptop. 'She dated a few different people when we were away, that I do know. She was pretty circumspect about it, but I know there were men and women. She loved everyone, I guess.'

'Well, I think it's probably more that she liked the people first, not necessarily their bodies,' Lila added.

'I guess so.' Nathan narrowed his eyes at the laptop. 'She was one of a kind, anyway, as I'm realising as I clear out her flat. Did you know she had a ouija board up there? There's all sorts of stuff. Some paintings I think might be originals. Boxes of letters and old photos. Cookbooks to the ceiling.'

'Wow. I mean, it doesn't surprise me, particularly.' Lila grinned. 'Serafina always struck me as a classic bohemian type. In the best way. I wish I was as cool as she was.'

Nathan looked up from his laptop and gave Lila an impenetrable look.

'You're cool in a different way. You're—' He was interrupted by a family entering the café noisily; the door banged open and there was a scuffle of kids suddenly running around, being called back to take their cardigans off and sit down. 'You better go over.'

'Just when you were going to tell me how cool I was.' Lila rolled her eyes. 'Another time, then.'

'For sure.' Nathan returned his gaze to his computer, but she watched him for a moment; he was smiling to himself, and she wondered what he would have said if they hadn't been interrupted.

Chapter Ten

The SUV drew up on the gravel drive outside a large country house. They'd needed a code to get into the gates at the entrance, then the taxi driver had dutifully followed the long drive as it swept through a grove of what looked like ancient cedars and redwoods, no doubt imported to Cornwall by a wealthy landowner hundreds of years ago.

'Here we are.' Nathan slid back the car door and hopped down from the step, holding a hand out to help Lila down.

'When you said we were catering a private party, I didn't think you meant *for the Queen*.' Lila followed him around to the back of the car where the driver had popped open the boot. Nathan was already leaning in to take out a number of boxes, cool bags and carrier bags full of ingredients and ready prepared cakes and pastries.

'Oliver's meeting us here, you said?' Nathan looked at his watch. 'I hope he'll be on time.'

'You're paying him pretty well, so I should think so.' Lila scanned the drive for signs of another car. 'He does tend towards lateness, though. His hair takes time to perfect.'

Nathan snorted.

'These people don't care about Oliver's hair,' he muttered, lifting a box carefully. 'I've got the scones in this one. Can you bring in the bag with the cream and all that stuff? We'll come out and get the rest in a minute once we know where we're setting up.'

'It was good of Oliver to help us, though, with the baking?' Lila replied pointedly as she hefted a hessian bag over one shoulder and a padded cool bag containing cream, butter and home-made strawberry jam. The cream and butter came from a local dairy, Gordon's – Lila hadn't known how creamy and delicious either could be until she'd moved to Magpie Cove. The farmer's family – the farmer himself, a hulking yet gentle guy of about fifty, and a couple of his equally tall and brawny sons – made deliveries of milk, cream, yoghurt and butter a couple of times a week. Serafina had bought all her dairy supplies from Gordon's, but Nathan had cancelled the café's order in the first week he'd taken over. Luckily, Lila had persuaded him that if they were going to cater a posh afternoon tea for some rich family or other, they couldn't rely on supermarket supplies.

It transpired that Nathan's grand plan to supplement the café was to use its premises for private catering. He'd got them this booking through some old friend – he was unforthcoming with the details – which required Lila to get a ton of baking done in under a week, on top of her college schedule and her shifts at the café. Ordinarily, she would have thought of asking Maude to fill at least some of the order, but things between them were still frosty, and Lila didn't want to ask in case it made things worse. After all, Maude did private catering now and again – Lila had even helped her on some of the jobs as work experience. It just felt like another way that Nathan was ruining Maude's business – on purpose, or not.

'It was, and it'll be great to have an extra pair of hands to serve, if he ever turns up,' Nathan grumbled as he knocked at the grand front door. The house looked like something out of a period drama: the wide, wooden double doors sat atop grand steps, and on each side, large, white-trimmed windows stretched the length of both floors. The external masonry was painted a delicate blue and a perfect green lawn stretched around the house. Lila wondered what the gardens were like at the back. Massive, probably. You never knew these places were even here unless you followed one of the long private drives off a small country road like they'd done earlier, and then found yourself at something straight out of an historical romance novel.

'I hope Maude doesn't find out about this.' Lila shifted her weight from one leg to the other: the bags were heavy. They heard footsteps approaching the door.

'Why?' Nathan frowned.

'She does this kind of catering.' Lila felt she needed to tell him, for the sake of transparency. 'I've helped her a few times.'

'Maude can get her own gigs,' Nathan replied, flatly. 'There's a limited customer base. Survival of the fittest. It's just healthy competition – that's how a free economy works.'

'Come on. This is Magpie Cove.' Lila rolled her eyes. 'When Maude finds out she'll be offended.'

'Oh, for Pete's sake! Anyone would think you didn't want the experience – or the extra money, I might add.' Nathan glared at her. 'You and your friend are students, need I remind you. I'm giving you the opportunity to be involved in a very high-quality private catering event. Isn't that something you're supposed to be training for?' Nathan hissed. 'I don't care what Maude may or may not feel. This is business.'

The door was opened by an attractive middle-aged woman wearing a crisp grey pencil skirt, forest-green blouse and black stilettos, standing in the doorway.

'Ah, Mr DaCosta? The catering? Perfect timing.' Lila suddenly felt dowdy in her catering whites. 'And your colleague? Welcome. I'm Sarah, the housekeeper; I'll show you where to set up.'

They followed Sarah into the house, her high heels clicking on a perfect white marble floor. Lila wondered if she ever lost her balance on such a slippery surface, especially in those heels. A housekeeper wearing what looked suspiciously like Louboutins wasn't quite what Lila had expected. She was cross with Nathan and wished she'd never come, even though the extra money was useful. Still, she thought to herself, she was here now, and Nathan was her boss. So she was stuck here.

'Just checking it's a party of twenty?' Nathan asked her as they traversed the long hall, hung with old-fashioned oil portraits intermixed with modern paintings. *Just that wall of art would probably pay for my flat*, Lila thought, admiring some of the pieces. Doors led off the hall to the left, mostly closed; as they got to the end, Sarah took a right turn and led them down another corridor and into a huge kitchen.

'Yes, twenty, although Mrs Henderson has probably invited more. She went to the golf club yesterday, so… Here we are! Please use whatever you need, and don't worry about cleaning up, I have staff that can do that.' Sarah looked Lila up and down somewhat critically. 'Is it just you serving? I thought there was going to be another server.'

'My name's Lila. Nice to meet you.' Lila gave the woman a deliberately bright smile. 'My colleague Oliver will be here soon.'

'I see. I take it you brought extras of everything, for the extra guests?' Sarah addressed Nathan rather than Lila. *So that's how it's going to be,* Lila thought. *Rude.*

'Err… not exactly…' Nathan looked uncharacteristically panicked. 'When I spoke to Mrs Henderson, she assured me the party was for twenty people.'

'Well, any good event business anticipates changes on the day and is prepared for them.' Sarah raised her eyebrow: an icy tone had entered her voice. 'I'm sure you agree?'

'A few extras are fine,' Lila interrupted. 'Oliver and I planned for additions when we were baking. We're actually the patissiers, rather than just servers. I thought that had been made clear in Nathan's email. So, as well as serve, we can speak to your guests about the provenance of the ingredients, the processes used in baking, and so on.' She gave Sarah what she hoped was an assertively pleasant look. 'And of course, we'll just add those extra guests onto our final invoice on an additional per head fee basis, which is twenty per cent more than for booked guests. I'm sure Mrs Henderson will have anticipated the additional fees when she invited her additional guests. As an experienced party host.'

Sarah blinked, then smiled wryly.

'Of course, Lila; when you have the final bill ready, just send it on. I'm looking forward to sampling some of your creations.'

'I certainly will, Sarah. Now, perhaps you can show Nathan where the tea will be staged? And I'll get on with putting the finishing touches on the pastries.' Lila turned to the spotless stainless-steel kitchen counter and started laying out a number of cake platters and a couple of vintage tiered cake stands. *Cheeky cow. I am not a waitress.* Lila glared at Sarah's back.

'Of course. Follow me, Nathan.' Sarah clicked away across the kitchen with Nathan following; she looked up, still cross, to see him grinning at her. She shot him a *what?* look until he looked away. Sarah, however, seemed very interested in Nathan – Lila watched as she stood to one side to let him walk in front of her, blatantly checking him out as he did so.

Nathan might have been a talented banker, but Lila doubted whether he could deal with twenty or more tipsy middle-aged rich women, all of whom were likely to find him very attractive indeed. She snorted in amusement as she finished unpacking the bags she'd brought in and headed out to get the rest and see if Oliver had turned up. If Sarah was anything to go by, then Mrs Henderson and her friends were going to eat Nathan alive.

Chapter Eleven

'You're cutting it fine.' Lila handed Oliver a box containing their beautiful hand-made pink raspberry macarons and a carefully packed Tupperware container of pastry horns that would shortly be filled with piped *crème anglaise*.

'Sorry, babes. Wanted to look my best. Plus, I swung by the hospital on my way to see Cyd and Betty. Dropped off that Victoria sponge that sank in the middle to the nurses' station.'

'Oh. How are Betty and Cyd?' Lila took the last of the cool bags from the boot of the taxi which had been patiently waiting when she and Nathan were inside. She tapped the driver's window. 'All done now, thank you! Pick up at six?'

The driver nodded and pulled away slowly back up the long drive. Oliver had parked his yellow Mini at a chaotic angle on the drive; Lila chose to ignore it. If she asked him to move it now, they'd get behind, and they already had a lot to do.

'They're all right. Nurse says Cyd can probably go home in a couple of weeks, but it did make me think about what we discussed. I really don't think they're getting the care they need at home, and it's just a matter of time before something else happens. Another fall or something…' He seemed to take notice of his surroundings for the first time. 'Blimmin' heck, missus, we're at Downton Abbey! I could have worn my Lady Violet earrings.'

'Hmm. Well, it's good to know Cyd's getting better, anyway.' Lila led Oliver up the imposing front steps. 'We'll think of something. But for now, we've got loads to do.' They trooped inside and down the hall, laden with bags. Oliver peeked into one room, and then casually opened one of the closed doors.

'Oi! You can't go in there!' Lila hissed.

'Why not?' He peered inside. 'Ooh, I like that sofa. I can just imagine watching *Drag Race* in there next to a roaring fire.'

Lila kicked his foot gently. 'Come on. Stop it.'

'You're no fun, Miss Bridges. This is the life I was born for.'

'Well, right now, you need to be born to assemble cream horns with me in the kitchen. And the sandwiches need making.'

'Jeez.' He followed her into the kitchen, where Nathan was taking several bottles of champagne from the fridge. 'Nathan, my darling, I'm pretty sure you shouldn't be stealing the champers.'

'Oh, you made it, then?' Nathan gave Oliver a flat stare. Lila glared at him; Oliver wasn't that late, and anyway, could he really afford to be mean to one of two people in the room who knew what they were doing? Nathan caught her stare and seemed to understand, because he nodded politely at Oliver. 'Good to see you. It turns out we have twenty-eight in the party and not twenty. Lila seems confident that we can cover that – can we?'

Oliver flapped his hand.

'Oh, don't worry about it, boss man, we got this. Go and mingle with the party. We'll start bringing the sandwiches and scones out in a minute.'

Nathan looked uncomfortable.

'It's fine, I'll stay here and help,' he muttered.

Oliver laughed. 'Why? What have they done to you?' he snorted, walking to the sink to wash his hands.

'Nothing.' Nathan set the last bottle on the work surface and wiped his hands on a cloth. 'They're just very… animated.'

Lila returned to slicing cucumber into thins and laying them expertly on the fresh granary bread they'd brought with them. They'd also planned smoked salmon and dill on rye bread as open sandwiches, roast beef and mustard on white and a heritage tomato with basil on gluten-free mini rolls.

'Here. Take over the sandwiches, will you?' She handed Oliver the knife. 'And let's just say our guests are women of a certain age who really like a drink with their afternoon tea.'

'Drunk already, are they?' Oliver's hands worked quickly and efficiently as he sliced tomatoes and laid them on the rolls, then arranged the smoked salmon on the rye bread.

'Seems like it.' Lila grinned at Oliver as she carefully piped the creamy filling into the chocolate-dipped cream horns and laid them carefully on the tiered platter.

'It's just not the kind of thing I'm used to,' Nathan replied primly.

'All right. Leave this to me, Nathan, baby.' Oliver finished the sandwiches, wiped his hands on the tea towel and picked up two platters.

'Down the hall. You'll hear them…' Nathan sounded positively haunted. Lila was desperate to giggle, and was avoiding meeting Oli's eyes: if she did, she knew she would erupt into gales of laughter. She picked up two of the multi-tiered cake stands on which she had arranged plain and fruit scones alongside a gluten-free batch she and Oli had baked yesterday, then followed her friend out of the kitchen.

If Nathan had quailed at the room of braying, glamorous middle-aged women quaffing champagne like it was going out of fashion, then Oliver sailed into the spacious, gleaming dining room like a seasoned, and extremely camp maître d'.

'Laaaadies! Good afternoon.' He leaned over the table, placing the sandwich trays down; Lila followed suit with the scones. 'Delighted to make your acquaintance. I'm Oliver and this is Lila: you can ask us for anything this afternoon, and we will do our best to bring it out for you.'

'Anything?' one of the women shouted out.

'Darling, as long as it's edible,' he shot right back, and the whole room laughed. 'Now, Miss Lila and I made all of the patisserie you'll be savouring, so if you have any questions, or want to tip us generously, then don't be shy. I'll tell you anything you want to know. The cream in our cream tea – the best scones in Cornwall, I might add – is from a local organic dairy farm. And let me tell you, that cream comes from some of the most wholesome beef in the county – and I'm not talking about the cows here, ladies.' He raised an eyebrow. 'All I'll say is those farm boys make me happy deep in my soul. Really, really deep down.' He grinned, as a huge laugh rang around the room again. Most women loved Oliver, and he was in his element.

Lila went back out for the rest of the first course, smiling to herself.

'What's going on out there? It sounds like Elvis in Las Vegas or something.' Nathan was lurking by the fridge, fiddling with his phone.

'Anyone would think you were hiding in here.' Lila gave him an amused look. 'It's just Oli doing what he does best.'

'Is he all right? One of them definitely touched my bum.'

'You don't know Oli. He'll be sitting on someone's lap by now. But in all seriousness, he's telling them about the gluten-free options... I hope. If you're going to stay in here, you can help me pipe these cupcakes. I didn't want to do it beforehand in case they got squashed. I don't have the right kind of box to transport them safely in.' Lila didn't add that Maude had some, but that she hadn't wanted to ask to borrow them.

'Um... okay, but I haven't done it before.' He looked nervous.

'Don't worry. All you have to do is squeeze and turn. See?' Lila demonstrated with a piping bag fitted with a silver nozzle. She piped one perfect cream cheese swirl of frosting on a Guinness and chocolate cake base, then handed the bag to Nathan.

He tried the first one, but the frosting came spiralling out faster than he expected and he was left with a huge pile of piping that fell off the cake.

'Whoops.' Lila giggled. 'Not so hard next time. Gentle. Turn the cake with your other hand if you like.'

He gave her a pained expression.

'It's all right for you. You've been doing this for ages.'

'I know, but you'll catch on. Try again.'

'It looks like white dog poop.' He glared at the cake. 'I really think you should take over.'

'I've got loads to do. You do it.' Lila started giggling again as Nathan piped another terrible topping. This time, he was too gentle.

'Rabbit droppings,' he said gloomily. 'Lila! Don't make me pipe any more.'

'Rabbit droppings?'

'Yes. Like, small bits that keep breaking off.'

She put down the gluten-free rolls and came to stand next to him. Awkwardly, she took his right hand in hers and squeezed the bag lightly. It was a strange sensation when someone else was holding it.

'Ooh.' Nathan started to chuckle now. 'That's weird.'

'Well, it's not supposed to be… I mean… I'm not supposed to be squeezing your bag for you,' she replied, trying to be sternly professional, but he caught her eye and they both started laughing.

'Heaven forbid.' Nathan raised his eyebrow at Lila, which just made her laugh more.

'You have to do it harder, but not too hard,' she tried to explain, and then realised how it sounded. 'Oh, come on. You know what I mean!'

'I'm not sure that I do. Explain it again for me,' he sniggered. Suddenly, it was like they were in Home Economics at school and Nathan had switched from grumpy, distant boss to a long-lashed boy with a million-watt grin that she could definitely develop a crush on.

'Okay. Maybe I'd better finish these.' Lila held out her hand for the piping bag and Nathan handed it to her gratefully.

'Thank goodness.' He wiped his eyes and grinned. 'I don't think I'm cut out for a life of icing cupcakes.'

'Maybe not. You can help with the champagne since you got it out – we don't want it getting warm.' Lila grinned back. She wished Nathan let that side of himself show more often – he was boyish, silly and kind of sweet. She liked it much more than his usually grimly serious self.

Nathan made a face. 'I'd rather stay in here.'

'Oh, don't be ridiculous. I'll protect you. We'll be in and out, I promise. Then you can help me with the patisserie. Something else, not piping,' she added.

'Fine, fine. It looks great, by the way. The food.' He picked up two bottles and followed her out of the kitchen. 'And I'm sorry I choked earlier, about the extra guests. I should have known you two had it under control.'

'Thanks. I appreciate that.' Lila led Nathan back into the dining room, where Oliver was now serenading the room with what sounded like 'Don't Rain on My Parade' from the musical *Funny Girl*. She placed the rest of the scones, cream, and jam down, with a separate cheese scone platter arranged around a soft pat of the gorgeous salted butter from Gordon's dairy.

'See? Perfectly under control,' she whispered, as they stood at the back of the room, watching Oliver play the heartstrings – and possibly other parts – of every privileged, demanding woman in that room.

'I take it all back.' Nathan shook his head in wonder. 'He's amazing.'

'Don't let him hear you say that.' Lila grinned. 'But, yes, he is.'

Chapter Twelve

'So, what I'm hearing is, because of my Barbra, we saved that afternoon tea from certain disaster.' Oliver poured his Italian meringue carefully from the food mixer bowl into his piping bag, secured the end with a clip and laid it carefully on his worktop.

Lila frowned, whisking her lemon curd in a copper pan, then testing it on the back of a cold spoon. They were making an intricate take on lemon meringue pie, a favourite of a highly regarded Michelin-star chef, and she wanted to get every stage just right. As soon as the curd started to thicken, she had to get it in the food mixer, add gelatine and butter and let it thicken even more. The finished result had four main elements, all of which were extremely delicate, and it would be so easy to lose concentration and ruin the whole thing. Oliver, in contrast to Lila's careful checking and double-checking every stage, seemed hardly to check the recipe at all.

'If that's what you want to hear, babe, then don't let me *rain on your parade*,' Lila replied, deadpan, her tongue between her teeth in concentration. 'I'm just happy we did it and got paid.'

'Haha. It's my signature song, don't be mean. And I have to admit some extra cash came in handy.' Oliver started squeezing lemons into a glass bowl. 'The adulation didn't go amiss, either.'

'Adulation,' Lila tutted. 'Your head couldn't get any bigger.'

'Shut up. It's the perfect size.'

'So, anyway, I wanted to catch up about Cyd and Betty. What d'you think? Shall we just agree a kind of rota – we can cover a few meals a week each? I mean, it's a stretch, but I want to do something.' Lila decided to change the subject, otherwise Oli would be going on about his adoring ladies for the whole day.

'Well, they do still get Meals on Wheels. It's just that it's not enough.' Oliver combined the ingredients for his lemon curd in a pan and set it on the heat. 'Why are you ahead of me, Lila Bridges? Are you cheating?'

'No. I'm just not talking as much as you.' Lila checked the consistency of her lemon curd and started to sieve it, as per the recipe's instructions. She had to get the curds into the freezer as soon as possible so they'd set: Jakob wanted the desserts presented perfectly by 5 p.m., and it was ten in the morning already. 'We just have to supplement what they're already getting. Even if we can take them up a loaf of bread, some fruit, cheese and cold meats, that would be a help.'

'I know,' Oliver mused. 'I just… I look at those women at the party, drinking champagne, mowing through our cakes, and it was just another day for them. And poor old Cyd and Betty are up in the hospital, practising being stoic. Not fair really, is it?'

'No.' Lila started to pour the curd into her individual prepared ramekins. 'But let's make a fuss of them when they come home, anyway.'

'Yes. They'd love that. A welcome home thing.' Oliver beamed. 'You're a good egg, Miss Bridges.'

'What about an oldies' supper club? Make sure Cyd and Betty have at least a few solid meals a week. And not just them – there's got to be quite a few elderly residents of Magpie Cove that would love a hot meal and a bit of a chat,' Lila mused.

'Well, yes, babes, but that's a huge commitment. It took us ages to prep for that afternoon tea. We don't have the time to do that every week. Or the money – because we'd be doing it for free.' Oliver shrugged. 'I can't see how we'd make it work.'

'Well, what about those rich housewives?' Lila said, taking the ramekins and putting them in the fridge. She turned back to Oliver. 'At the party. I'm sure they'd like to support the elderly – if they knew how little they're living on, they'd be shocked.'

'Maybe,' Oliver mused. 'But I'm not sure Nathan would like us turning up at his client's house with our begging bowls. Even if it was for charity.'

She put her hands on her hips. 'Perhaps. But what if Nathan doesn't know? He doesn't own them. There's nothing to stop us fundraising on our own.'

'Or, my dear feisty friend, you could ask Nathan to chip in?' Oliver suggested, mimicking her hands-on-hip stance. 'He's got a business background and he now owns a catering business. He's bound to have some advice. And a spare few bob lying around.'

'You just want an excuse to talk to Nathan,' Lila teased, but she was considering it. Maybe Nathan was the obvious person to help them? After all, he hadn't minded about her giving Cyd and Betty free food when she thought he would object.

'Well, duh.' Oliver gave an exaggerated shrug. 'But what harm would it do to ask, eh?'

'I guess it's worth a try.'

They continued working at their desserts in silence for a minute. Lila still wondered whether she could talk to Oliver about why she'd come to Magpie Cove, but there never seemed to be a good moment. They were either at college or visiting Cyd and Betty and neither was right. How did you even start talking about such a thing? Oliver was a caring person; that was obvious in the way that he regarded the old ladies. But Lila still felt a resistance. And did she even really want to? Things were perfect as they were.

'Penny for them?' Oliver looked up from his tart-making and waggled his eyebrows. 'Thinking about Nathan in his designer suits? Or... out of them?'

Lila shook her head. 'No. Nothing like that.' She looked back down at her work.

'Still waters run deep.' Oliver sighed dramatically. 'He's just like you. I must be drawn to the strong, silent type.'

Lila looked up, astonished. 'I'm not the strong, silent type!' She was anything but, surely.

'Oh, you go ahead thinking that, Miss Bridges,' her friend tutted. 'I know you've got stories. One day, I'll get them out of you. My very own Elizabeth Taylor.' He took his pastry, filled with curd, to the freezer and came back, wiping his hands. 'I can see the drama in your aura. Beautiful, yet tortured by your past. I can see it, missus.'

'I don't know what you mean.' Lila felt herself blushing. It was like Oliver had read her mind.

'Oh, you do.' Her friend patted her hand. 'I'm here when you're ready to spill it. And in the meantime, I've got plenty of drama to fill you in on. Did I tell you about my recent date with the online guy?' Oliver launched into a story about one of his recent romantic exploits; Lila listened as she worked on her dessert. She hadn't known that she was apparently projecting something that made her seem tortured. She thought she was so controlled, so easy and pleasant and noncommittal, like she always had been. All the things you needed to be to float at the edges of friendship without getting close to anyone; without being noticed.

But Oliver *had* noticed her, and could see something in her that she'd fought so hard to hide. Did that mean that she'd unconsciously let her guard down, or that Oliver was particularly perceptive?

Or was it that for the first time in a long time, she'd let herself have a real friend? Alice was far away in London, and had been the only other person who had persevered long enough to insist on being Lila's friend. Oliver, too, had not taken no for an answer. Despite all Lila's attempts to make him into a pleasant acquaintance, Oliver cared about her, and refused to let her go. It was an unfamiliar feeling for Lila: it made her a little panicky, to think that anyone wanted to know her secrets. But there was also a glimmer of hope there, too: that if someone finally knew the real her, they would still love her.

Chapter Thirteen

All day Lila waited for the right time to ask Nathan about the money for the supper club, but it never quite seemed to materialise.

For a start, Nathan didn't come into the café until half past ten, which was about normal. Lila usually opened up on her solo days, and could handle the breakfast customers on her own. There was still a sharp decline in people popping in for a morning coffee and croissants like they used to – obviously because of Nathan's new rules. No one wanted to be hurried through a morning flick through the papers and a delicious coffee whilst they listened to the smooth jazz Lila tended to play in the mornings. Rovina, Eric and some of the other pensioners still came in for their breakfast, but Cyd and Betty remained in the hospital. Lila had called through to the ward the day before and had a chat with Betty, who sounded chipper as usual, but Lila detected strain in her voice. It was exhausting, being in hospital, never mind if you were already weak.

When he'd finally come in, Nathan was on a phone call that seemed to take hours. When he finally emerged from the back room and put an apron on, the lunch customers had started coming in and they were both busy taking and preparing orders. There was an art show in town and they were busier than usual: good news for the café, especially as new customers were more likely to take the new rules in their stride. They hadn't ever known the café under Serafina's free and easy ownership, after all – though some people still asked after her. Lila thought that those people must have been to Magpie Cove before and noticed the difference.

By the time the lunch rush was over and Lila had time to start stacking the dishwasher and restocking the cakes on the counter display, Nathan had set up his laptop on one of the café tables and was tapping furiously at a document he had open. *It's now or never,* she thought, approaching the table with a cup of tea which she placed beside him.

'Thanks.' He looked up briefly, but then stared back at the laptop as if it held the answers to the Bermuda Triangle and Area 51 combined. 'Sorry. Accounts for the café are all over the place. Trying to get them into some semblance of order before I have to do a tax return.'

'You're welcome. Umm... about that. Well, not the café accounts. But—'

'I know. Your job.' He sat back in his chair. 'Okay. As I said before, I can definitely keep the café open for two more months, but it remains to be seen if it can remain profitable after that. A few more days like today would help, mind you. Art show, did you say it was?'

'Yes. It's an annual one held at the museum. Small, but well thought of. The good thing about being the only café in town is that everyone comes here for lunch.' Lila played with her amber ring. 'Two more months is great, but it still isn't long enough to see me to the end of the course. Four months would be better.'

'What would be better is if Magpie Cove held more art shows.' Nathan peered at a scrawled-in notebook and made a face. 'Sorry, I just can't commit to that. I mean, hopefully, sure, but... honestly, these records... I don't know how she managed to keep the café going all these years. It's like she was just giving food away.'

'Look, I'll stay those two months, I need the work.' She'd just have to make it happen. 'Actually, though, that wasn't what I wanted to talk about,' Lila began again. 'I wanted to talk to you a bit about the elderly customers we have. You remember them?'

'Mmm-hmm,' Nathan replied distractedly as he entered a number in the spreadsheet he was working on.

'Well, the thing is, they're getting ever more frail, as are a lot of the elderly in the village. Serafina's senior citizen breakfast used to be an important part of their weekly routine – both as a reliable and cheap hot meal a few times a week but also as a way to socialise. It can get really lonely if you don't have a reason to go out,' Lila continued.

'They're welcome to continue coming in for breakfast. You know that.' Nathan didn't take his eyes off the screen.

'Yes. It's just that… it's getting harder for some of them to make it to the café nowadays, so Oliver and I were thinking of doing something else for them. A supper club. But we'd need some help.'

'A supper club?' Nathan was still looking at his spreadsheet.

'Yes. The thing is, most of the elderly people in the village get a Meals on Wheels service, but something's happened to it recently and they're hardly getting any food at all. Nathan, these people are starving.'

Nathan picked up the notebook again and frowned at it.

'Just doesn't make sense,' he muttered.

'Are you listening to me?' Lila raised her voice. 'Please. Nathan?'

'Lila, these accounts are difficult to understand, and I really need some peace and quiet right now. Sorry, I don't mean to be rude.' He gave her a surprisingly sweet smile. 'Can we talk about this later? I know the old people mean a lot to you.'

She was slightly taken aback at the fact that he had, at least, understood how much Cyd and Betty did mean to her, and seemed to care.

'Later?'

'Why don't we go for a drink after closing? I could do with a change of scene, and I expect you could too. Tell me all about it then. Okay?'

'Oh. Okay.' Lila was too surprised to comment. 'At the pub, you mean?'

'Sure. Haven't been there for years.'

'Err… right.' She ran a hand through her hair. *A drink? At the pub? Like… as friends?* She was suddenly glad she wore dresses to work and had done her hair this morning.

'Looking forward to it.' His eyes twinkled for a moment, meeting hers. There was a flash of something between them… a kind of frisson that wasn't evident before. *What is happening?* Lila wondered as she returned his gaze, then looked away.

'Well, I'd better…' She flapped the tea towel tucked into her apron's waistband at the café.

'Right.' He held her gaze for half a second longer than felt normal, then looked back at his spreadsheet. 'I'll be ready for a drink after this.'

The Crown and Feathers was a few streets away from the café; a small corner establishment that had been there for as long as anyone could remember. It didn't do food or music or cater for children. Serafina had once commented that it remained an old-fashioned haven for men who wanted to escape from their families. It was the type of pub where, when you walked in, everyone turned around to look at you.

'Some things never change,' Nathan murmured to Lila as they stood in the doorway, meeting the stares of the few regulars that clustered around the small, varnished wood tables and leaned against the sticky bar.

Lila had only been in once before, with Oliver, which had prompted a similar response. They'd spent the evening drinking double gin and tonics, eating crisps and giggling at the regulars.

Fortunately, Oli was so good with people that, rather than stay the outcasts in the corner, by the end of the night they'd all somehow ended up arm-in-arm, singing 'Land of Hope and Glory'. Not that anyone was sober enough by that point to remember any of the verses.

'Evenin', miss. What can I get yer?' The jowly, bearded landlord from last time didn't seem to be here. Instead, a curvaceous barmaid in her twenties wearing a low-cut top and jeans appraised Nathan with a definite gleam in her eye. 'An' sir? Don't get many come in here wearin' a suit. Made my day, that has.'

She leaned provocatively on the bar and smiled widely at Nathan. Lila darted a look at him and was half amused to see that he looked a little uncomfortable at the barmaid's obvious flirting.

'Pint of bitter, thanks. Lila?'

'Glass of white wine, please. Dry, if you have it.'

'I do.' The barmaid turned around to a small glass-fronted fridge and selected a green bottle, uncorked it and poured a generous glass. 'And a pint for Mr Stockbroker,' she added, pulling rich brown bitter with a thick white head into a pint glass.

Nathan paid, and they sat down at the same corner table she'd shared with Oliver.

'Thanks for the drink,' Lila said. It was very quiet in the pub and she had the strong feeling that everyone was going to listen to their conversation. She felt uncomfortable, and wished they'd stayed in the café and had a coffee or something. She gulped a third of the wine in one go to settle her nerves.

'You're welcome. Cheers.' He tilted his glass at her.

'That barmaid likes you.' Lila felt a slight buzz from the wine. She took another sip.

'Don't be ridiculous.' Nathan looked over at the bar and then back to Lila. 'She's just being friendly. That's her job.'

'She didn't say my outfit made her day, *Mr Stockbroker*,' Lila added in a faux-breathy voice. Really, she didn't know what had come over her. She would make that kind of joke with Oli, but Nathan just gave her a slightly amused look and said nothing. *Awkward.*

She had got used to Nathan's smart attire to some extent, but she had to admit that he did look good in his dark navy suit and white shirt underneath. He wasn't wearing a tie, and the shirt was open at the neck where she could just glimpse a tuft of chest hair. She found herself wondering what he would look like without the shirt on at all, and then stopped herself. Whatever the barmaid had thought was catching.

'Hmm. So, what was it that you wanted to talk about?' Nathan redirected the conversation adroitly, but not before Lila detected a slight blush.

'Oh, right. Oli and I want to start a supper club for the elderly people in Magpie Cove,' she began, making herself focus. 'We want to do maybe a weekly dinner delivery. We can't do every day, but perhaps once or even twice a week we can get a good dinner and a chat to those that can't get out – and for those that can still get out and about, a night where they can have dinner and catch up with their friends.'

'Okay… I mean, I was thinking about what you said earlier. I suppose we could keep the café open later one evening a week if we've got enough customers who are going to buy dinner.' Nathan took another sip of his bitter. The barmaid turned on a crackly radio and gave the pub some much needed background noise: Lila was relieved. At least now they could talk without everyone having to listen.

'Oh. That's a nice offer, but…' She thought about it for a moment. It *was* a nice offer, and it was nice that Nathan had come up with any solution at all. She'd only mentioned it this afternoon. Still, she pressed on – there was no point in not explaining the idea. 'That's not what I meant. Though that is a kind thought. I mean, I want this to be free for the elderly. Charitable.'

'Oh. I see. And who's paying for it? Someone has to pay, somewhere along the line.' Nathan sat back in his chair.

'Well, you're my first port of call. I thought you might be interested in donating. As a local businessman.' Lila sipped her wine.

'I'm in business, Lila. I'm not a philanthropist,' he replied shortly, a cloud crossing his face. 'Is this what you wanted? Butter me up with a drink and then ask for money?'

'Well, you suggested the pub, and bought the drinks, so, no,' Lila replied, a little crossly. 'Actually, I thought more that businesses have budgets for charitable giving.' She tried to keep the irritation out of her voice. 'And since this benefits the community you work in, that has to benefit the café?'

'Tell me how giving my money away benefits the café. I'm all ears.' He raised an eyebrow. Oh, he was infuriating! *Just when I'm starting to like you, and you seem like a nice person, you act like you're in* The Wolf of Wall Street *or something*, Lila thought. Well, if she was honest, that was probably an exaggeration. But *still.*

'It'll make you look good. Show people in Magpie Cove that you care about the community. People respond to things like that. People care about the elderly, you know,' Lila snapped.

'Then why aren't they helping them already?' Nathan steepled his fingers together and leaned his elbows on the table. 'Look, Lila. It's a lovely idea. But I can't fund what sounds like an ongoing soup kitchen. I've got a business to run, and at the moment I don't know if I can make it work at all. If you come to me with a business plan, I can look it over and help you where I can. But in terms of money, no. I mean, how much are you asking for? How many people does this supper club serve? Who is making the food and distributing it? Where will you source your ingredients? Have you worked out any of that?'

Lila felt dejected. 'No,' she snapped again. 'We haven't got that far yet. We just thought—'

'I know you want to help Cyd and Betty. Why don't you and Oli just do their shopping a couple of times a week, make them a few cakes, that kind thing? I'm sure that would make a big difference,' he suggested.

'Yes, but it isn't just Cyd and Betty,' Lila tried to explain. 'It's sad knowing that there are old people that hardly see anyone week to week. They might be starving and no one would ever know.'

'I understand,' Nathan said, his tone softening, briefly squeezing her hand across the table. 'And it says so much that you care as much as you do. But you can't just become a one-woman social services.'

'Why not?' People do things like this all the time.' Lila raised her chin, resisting his sympathy. She was angry. She wanted to help. There wasn't anything wrong in that.

'Maybe. But those people aren't studying for qualifications and working at the same time just to keep a roof over their heads. This kind of thing takes time, energy and money. You might have the energy, but I don't think you have the time to do it justice. Or the money.'

'That was where you came in,' Lila repeated.

'Yes, and I've explained how I can help,' Nathan replied patiently. 'I'm happy to help you plan and look at the possibilities. All I'm saying is don't rush in with both feet. At the moment you don't know what you need and for how long and how it would even work. Do that first, at least.'

'If we came to you with a decent plan, would you help us with some funding then?' Lila took a long sip of wine.

'Maybe, but I'm not promising anything. Okay?'

'Okay.'

There was a silence where neither of them knew what to say. Lila didn't feel as discouraged as she had earlier: in fact, if she was being totally honest, she had come to Nathan woefully underprepared. He'd been nice enough to point that out without making her feel like a *total* idiot, though it wasn't far off. Lila conceded that it was, in fact, the second time that Nathan could have made her feel stupid and hadn't, remembering when she'd stolen food from the café for Cyd and Betty.

Nathan took a long draught of his bitter. His hands were long-fingered and strong. For a moment, she found herself imagining how they would feel, stroking her skin, then berated herself instantly for the thought. *What was wrong with her?*

'So, how's the course coming along?' he asked.

'Oh. Good, I think.' Lila realised that her glass was almost empty. 'We have an end-of-year project coming up, and I haven't even thought about it yet. I'm supposed to plan and make an event cake, like a wedding cake, but it could be a really elaborate birthday or corporate thing. Something big that demonstrates the techniques we've learnt. It has to be a theme that means something to you. I have no ideas at the moment.'

'It's a shame you can't combine that with your supper club idea.' Nathan looked thoughtful. 'But I don't suppose supper clubs for the elderly call for elaborate wedding cakes. Speaking of events, by the way, I've booked in a Sunday event at the café. I don't need you to do any catering, but I hope you don't mind helping serve? Double time, of course.'

'Oh. Yes, I guess so.' The extra money would come in handy.

'Good. The art show organisers called me up this afternoon? They're doing some kind of shindig and called the café to see if they could have it there.'

'Shindig? I'm sorry, is it the 1970s?' She raised her eyebrows. Was she flirting? She might have been flirting. She hadn't meant to, but there was something nice about teasing Nathan. He seemed to like it.

'You know what I mean. Drinks. They're going to hang some of their paintings and walk around and talk about them, I don't know. What do artists do?' His cheeks reddened. 'It's not exactly my thing.'

'No, I guess not.' Lila grinned and downed the last of her wine: Nathan was still only halfway through his pint. 'Another?'

'No, I'm fine, though I can get you one.' He stood up as if to go to the bar.

'No, no, I'm fine too,' she lied. She actually really fancied another glass, but it felt wrong to be getting slowly tipsy while her boss – her very attractive boss that other women seemed to admire – stayed sober. She didn't want him to think she was some kind of lush.

'Are you sure? It's no trouble. I've never been much of a drinker, so I know I'm probably not as fun company as some people,' he added, sitting back down and taking off his jacket, draping it on the back of the chair. 'How long have you and Oliver been friends?'

'We met on the course, so… what, nine months, I guess.'

'He's a good friend of yours?' Nathan observed.

'Sure.' Lila wondered where this was going. Did Nathan think that she and Oliver were romantically involved? Surely he couldn't have assumed that, given Oli's Barbra Streisand medley at the afternoon tea. 'Oli is a lot of fun,' she added, not knowing what she wanted to say exactly. 'But… I find it hard to talk about some things. To anyone.'

'I'm a good listener.' Nathan's voice was quiet and suddenly somehow raw. Lila met his gaze, and something passed between them again. She couldn't say exactly what it was, but there was an intensity in his look that made her feel… tingly.

'Another time, maybe.' She wasn't going to talk about what had happened in a pub full of listening ears. She wasn't sure why she'd even said that about Oli in the first place: it wasn't any of Nathan's business how she felt about her new best friend. It was probably the wine.

He seemed to come to a decision. 'Let me walk you home, in that case.' He moved behind her and tried to pick up her coat from the back of her chair. However, Lila was leaning against it and hadn't quite realised what he was doing, so him pulling her coat out from under her made her jerk forwards and knock her glass over. Fortunately, it was empty.

'Oh God. I'm so sorry.' Nathan gave an uncharacteristic yelp and dropped her coat. 'I was just trying to be gentlemanly… are you okay?'

Lila stood up, grinning.

'I'm fine. Don't worry. I wouldn't have missed that yelp for the world.'

'Agh! Sorry. I'm all fingers and thumbs tonight.' He held out the coat and helped her on with it. His hand brushed her shoulder, and that same tingle of electricity she'd felt from before travelled from the spot his fingers had touched, down her spine. 'Wait, what? I don't yelp.'

'You definitely yelped. Like a lamb or a baby rabbit or something.' Lila giggled.

'No, I didn't!' He pretended not to know what she was talking about. 'Do the noise, then.'

Lila made a passable imitation of the yelp, and Nathan laughed.

'That is not what I did. That sounded like a fox mating.'

'Hey, don't shoot the messenger.' Lila shrugged. She looked around them and realised that everyone in the pub was staring at them. 'Maybe we better—'

'Yeah. I've probably kept you out too long as it is.' Nathan followed her gaze and cleared his throat.

It was a sweet thing to say, though Lila knew it was only perhaps seven o'clock.

'I won't turn into a pumpkin just yet,' she joked.

'Ah. I should have asked for a dance from the beautiful princess rather than take her to a... rather sticky, old man's pub,' Nathan murmured as he walked out after her. Lila snorted a laugh.

'A beautiful princess?'

'Of course. Who else would you be?'

'Not a randy fox, that's for sure.'

They stood in the evening sun, outside the pub. The street was quiet, and Lila could hear the sea birds that hovered over the coastline: gulls, magpies, cormorants sometimes. She didn't quite know how to reply. Was Nathan DaCosta flirting with her? It seemed totally unlikely, yet he wasn't the kind of person who would use outrageous compliments as a kind of conversational flourish like Oli did. She cleared her throat and turned up the street, towards her flat.

'You really don't have to walk me home,' she said, but felt a glow of excitement in her belly when he turned the same way to walk with her.

'Nonsense.' He grinned, putting his hands in his trouser pockets.

They walked up the street in silence. Nathan seemed content for them to walk quietly together like this, and after a minute of feeling uncomfortable, Lila began to get used to it. It seemed enough to look up and catch his eye and smile now and again:

she didn't have to try to impress him with her witty repartee – *or, lack of it*, she thought.

'Well, here I am.' They'd reached her flat. 'See you Saturday.'

'See you then.' He shuffled his feet, looking slightly uneasy. 'Have a good day at college.'

'Thanks.' She wondered what he was waiting for.

'Lila?' He looked more nervous. What was wrong? Was he going to sack her? She shouldn't have asked him for money, it had clearly created an uncomfortable atmosphere between them – apart from the whole animal yelp thing. She wasn't even sure what that was, only that – like when she'd show him how to pipe a cupcake that time – they'd ended up in fits of giggles and it was… nice.

'Yes?'

'I…' He stepped closer to her and met her eyes with a meltingly soft stare. Lila felt her footing shift to face him more directly: it was automatic, as was the tilt of her head to his. *He's going to kiss me,* she realised. *Oh.*

'Lila…'

'Yes?' she breathed. Some barrier had been crossed, some transformation had taken place and Nathan DaCosta had morphed from distant, unemotional boss to shy boy about to kiss her. She wasn't sure that she could trace the moment when it had happened, but suddenly, things felt very different.

Stranger still, she responded automatically, instinctively. She wanted Nathan to kiss her. There was a chemistry between them. She wasn't immune to Nathan's good looks, but it was more than that, it always had been for her when she liked someone. There had been occasional moments since she'd known him where she wondered whether he was flirting with her, and now, a whole new Nathan had suddenly appeared – one who made her stomach feel weak and made her feel pleasantly nervous. It was *the feeling*, and she had rarely felt it before.

Nathan closed his eyes and leaned in. Lila's eyes fluttered closed; she felt the light touch of his lips on hers. Sweetness suffused her body.

Just then, a car horn blared and Lila was jolted back to reality. She opened her eyes and stepped back from the kiss; a car of teenage boys zoomed past, closely avoiding clipping the side mirrors of the vehicles parked on the side of the narrow street. They shouted something indecipherable at Nathan and Lila before they drove off, laughing.

'Sorry.' Nathan frowned, wiping his mouth with the back of his hand. 'I shouldn't have done that.'

I don't have bad breath, Lila thought, suddenly annoyed. It was obvious that Nathan regretted kissing her – or, *almost* kissing her. One car of teenage boys shouldn't have kept him from trying again if he really wanted to – if he hadn't realised it was a giant mistake the moment he'd done it. *Well, that's just fine*, she thought, defensive. *I didn't want to kiss him either. I would have been perfectly happy going home after work: it was him that asked me out for a drink. Who insisted on walking me home. Who almost kissed me.*

'Fine. See you Saturday.' She turned around and climbed the steps to the blue front door without looking back, letting herself in and slamming it behind her. How dare he make her feel so awkward when it was him that had led her on? Now he wanted to forget anything ever happened. *Fine.* That was more than fine. Fineness personified. Fine baked into a cake. He could take his sweet, gentle kiss and stuff it up his well-tailored behind.

She was more than happy to keep things all business where Nathan DaCosta was concerned.

Chapter Fourteen

'I can't believe I'm doing this.' Oliver rolled his eyes dramatically.

Lila giggled. 'Yeah. Who needs a business plan? All we needed was two badly fitting leotards and some feather boas. Hold still.' She finished painting Oliver's face white and carefully glued on some thick black fake eyelashes, then adorned her own. Last, she handed him a cartoonish yellow duck's beak with an elastic loop.

In truth, she was pretty nervous, too, but the sight of Oliver dressed as a swan – complete with a white tutu and tights – was so entertaining that she'd half forgotten she was about to go on stage and make a complete idiot of herself. Before she'd met him, she would never have done anything like this. Even now, she had major reservations, but the fact that they were fundraising to feed the elderly in the village made it tolerable. Every time she thought she might back out, she imagined what it must be like to eat a ham slice and a single new potato for dinner. Making a fool of herself was worth it.

Obviously, it had been Oliver's idea. They'd been sitting in the college café after class, going over ideas for how they could make money to afford to make dinners for ten Magpie Cove residents on a regular basis. As well as herself and Cyd, Rovina and Eric, Betty had given Lila the phone numbers of six other pensioners in the village who she thought would be appreciative of a hot meal and a chat once or twice a week.

Lila estimated that meant a hundred and twenty dinners would be required if they were going to run it for a trial period, plus things like foil containers to transport them in. If the plan took off, they'd need much more equipment, like hot plates and special bags to keep the food warm. For now, if they could raise £500, that would cover the meals for three months, if Lila and Oliver chipped in a little themselves too. They couldn't afford to add much, because they already spent everything on bills and rent every month.

If we were top chefs, babes, Oliver had pointed out, *we could just do this out of our own massive salaries. But we're pastry students. So, we need a bit of help.*

Of all places, it was the tacky-floored old man's pub that had let them host their revue. Perhaps it had been that night when everyone ended up singing 'Land of Hope and Glory'; Lila didn't know. Maybe the regulars were more into show tunes than they let on. But when the laconic barmaid at the end of the phone had agreed that she and Oliver could come and sing some songs and generally prat about for charity, Lila had taken it and not asked questions.

'Ready?' She stood back and inspected her handiwork. They'd both slicked their hair back with gel to add to dramatic effect. The false eyelashes made her eyelids feel heavy, but apart from that, this was as ready as she'd ever be.

'All set, babes.' Oliver stood up from where he'd been leaning on the edge of the sink in the ladies' toilet. 'Let's do it.'

Lila peeked her head out of the door to the bathroom, caught the barman's eye and waved. The pub was packed. They'd invited everyone they could think of at short notice: Lila had been asking people at the café plus people from college, and Oliver had called some of the numbers he'd been given by the Real Housewives of St Ives, as he called them. The pub had only had one Sunday free, so it had given them just a few days to organise it all. It was a shame Cyd and Betty were still in the hospital: Lila knew they would have loved an opportunity to see Oliver perform.

'And now, ladies and gentlemen, for your entertainment this evening, in aid of the elderly of Magpie Cove, the Crown and Feathers is pleased to announce – for one night only – A Night with Barbra Streisand: or, Two Pastry Cooks in Search of a Melody!'

There was applause and a few excited yelps.

'That's us, then.' Lila took a deep breath. 'I think the Real Housewives are out in force. And it sounds like they're on the sauce already.' Her phone buzzed; Nathan was calling her. She turned the phone off, slipping it into her bag. Nathan could wait until tomorrow.

'Good.' Oliver pulled up his tights and slicked back his hair with his hand. 'The tipsier they get, the more we make.'

Lila didn't remember much from the performance itself. They'd started with 'His Love Makes Me Beautiful' from *Funny Girl*, the song in which Barbra Streisand's character plays a comical swan queen, followed by a rendition of 'Memory' from *Cats*, then 'My Man', 'The Way We Were' and 'Happy Days Are Here Again' for an upbeat finish – Lila had pointed out that all Oliver's favourite Barbra songs were about being broken-hearted, so they needed to end on a high.

Still, it seemed to go well. They'd asked for £5 admission at the door and, after the songs, Lila and Oliver held a raffle for the promise of a bespoke event cake one of them would make, an afternoon's patisserie lesson and a set of Barbra Streisand DVDs, kindly donated by Oliver, who had pointed out to Lila that you could stream Barbra anytime you wanted nowadays, anyway.

As Oliver ushered the last of the tipsy housewives out of the pub, Lila opened the donations jar and counted the money. She'd estimated they'd probably made about £150 from the door, and someone had bid £100 for the patisserie lesson and £150 for the bespoke cake – which, in fact, was a bargain and a half, considering how long it took to make them, not even taking into account the ingredients. If her maths was correct, that would make them around £400, which wasn't too far off their target.

'Good night's work for you, maid.' The barman nodded at the jar as she counted the notes. 'Good night at the bar, too. Your friends can come again,' he chuckled. 'Might need to get a bit more gin in for next time, mind. An' the sparklin' wine took a bit of a seein' to as well.'

'Mmm-hmm.' Lila didn't want to lose count. She'd got to £400 already and there seemed to be quite a lot more in the jar. Five hundred, six hundred... she looked up in amazement at Oliver as he walked over, his face paint streaked with sweat and lipstick on his cheek.

'Oli. There's...' She looked back at the piles of cash on the bar. 'There's around £700 here. And I haven't finished counting.'

'Seven hundred?' Oliver looked at the cash and back at her. 'Are you kidding?'

'No. Looks like your housewives enjoyed themselves.' Lila laughed in disbelief. 'This is amazing! This means we can do it. Start, at least.'

'Okay. I'll come round to yours next week and we can make a plan about what we can do, since we got more than we expected.'

Lila looked at the notes piled up on the bar again, still not quite believing her eyes. 'We need to work out menus, food suppliers... I need to think about it.'

'Well, if it feeds ten pensioners for a few months, it's worth it as a start, right?' Oliver encased Lila in a hug. 'We did it, Miss Bridges! Barbra would be so proud.' He picked her up off the bar stool and swung her around. 'We're going to be SO TIRED!' he screamed.

'But it's going to be SO WORTH IT!' Lila yelled, wrapping her arms around Oliver's neck and kissing him on the cheek. 'Thank you. For being so fabulous and having such brilliant ideas. I'd never have done this without you.'

Oliver put her down, grinning. 'Thank YOU for being my muse. The Neil Diamond to my Barbra.' He grinned. 'You were great tonight.'

'Oh, I was terrible. You were the star of the show.' Lila scrunched her face up, thinking about it. 'I can't really even sing.'

'You can! And I saw you playing up to the audience in "The Way We Were". You're a natural. Barry, are you still serving? I could murder a pint.' Oliver smiled beatifically at the barman.

'Right you are, Barbra.' Barry nodded. Lila laughed, amazed. Oliver really could work his magic anywhere.

'See, Miss Bridges? All this time, you thought Magpie Cove was a backwater Cornish village, and instead, it was a thriving cultural oasis,' Oliver said, demolishing his beer in four large gulps.

'I'm more of a fan o' *Yentl* than *Funny Girl*, but Miss Streisand's certainly welcome here any night o' the week.' Barry nodded again, wiping a glass and lining it up neatly behind the bar.

'See what I mean? People can always surprise you.' Oliver beamed at the barman.

'They certainly can,' Lila replied, looking at the piles of money on the bar.

Chapter Fifteen

There was a CLOSING sign in the window of Maude's Fine Buns. Lila frowned; she was pretty sure she hadn't noticed the sign before. She dashed across the road and pushed open the door to the small bakery.

'Morning, my love. Seen the sign, I take it?'

Maude gave Lila a weary grimace from where she stood behind the counter, bagging up some loaves of granary bread she'd just put through the old-fashioned slicer. She was only in her early forties, but today she looked tired, and much older than her years.

'You're closing? What do you mean? Like, temporarily?' Lila was confused.

'Permanent, I'm afraid. Shutting up shop. Not what I expected, but there you have it.'

'Why? I thought you were doing all right.'

'I was, before your boss stopped orderin' my cakes.' Maude sniffed. 'You have to sell a lot of baps 'n' millionaire's shortbread to stay afloat. But, no, it ain't that. I had a loan when I opened, but now, with the rents just gone up, I can't make ends meet. I was only just survivin' before. Sorry I didn't make it to your do last night. I was a bit under the weather.'

'Oh, that's fine, don't worry.' Lila shifted her weight uneasily from one foot to the other. She hadn't expected Maude to come anyway, since things were still pretty tense between them. 'What do you mean, your rent? Magpie Cove's cheap for renters. That's why I came here.'

'I thought you would have known, my love, what with working at the café. Now that Serafina's gone, the new owner of all her property has put the rents up. Across the board.'

'Serafina's property? What are you on about?' Lila ran her hand through her hair and pulled at a knot. 'Are you saying she was... your landlord?'

'Landlady, I s'pose. And yes. Serafina owned quite a few of the shops and places hereabouts. This place, the butcher's, some of the houses facing the beach, even the art gallery.' Maude laid out a row of spectacular-looking iced doughnuts in the glass counter: pink icing with raspberry jam and dried raspberry on the top, chocolate berliners, long doughnuts filled with vanilla custard and drizzled with chocolate. She handed a raspberry one to Lila. 'Here. For shock. On the 'ouse. If I could afford rent in St Ives I'd take my fine buns over there an' hike my prices up for that posh lot. I don't do a bad sourdough, though I say it myself. But it's just too much.'

Lila took the doughnut and bit into it: the soft dough and the sharp raspberry jam went some way to helping with the surprise, but she still didn't entirely understand what Maude was talking about. 'Serafina owned the art gallery? And the butcher's? She never said anything about that.'

'Owned the buildings, not the businesses. I knew, 'cause when I got here, it was 'er what showed me around the place. But she didn't want me tellin' people, an' I respected 'er wishes. She said to me that day she owned a fair bit o' property but she didn't like to let people know 'cause it'd make them think differently of 'er. Not sure how many others know.'

'Oh.' Lila had always thought that her boss was probably running on a shoestring, based on the number of handouts and favours she did for others: Nathan's reaction to the accounts the other day surely suggested that was the case. Now, her generosity made a bit more sense.

Serafina routinely gave away food that wasn't anywhere near out of date – Lila had accompanied her a few times making deliveries to some of the poorest families in the village, as if they'd put in an order and she was filling it. Lila also knew for a fact that Serafina catered birthday parties for many of the children in those families and generally 'forgot' to ask for payment.

'So… she was wealthy?' Lila asked, through a mouthful of doughnut.

'I'd say so. Though not half as much as she could've been. The rents in Magpie Cove 're cheap compared with everywhere else hereabouts. She never put the rent up, I heard. So families could cope. Businesses like me had a chance.' Maude shook her head. 'She were one of a kind, that one, God bless her.'

'I had no idea,' Lila mused. 'So… who's put the rents up now?'

'The new owner. Her son, innit? Didn't waste no time, either.' Maude rolled her eyes.

'Nathan?' Lila couldn't quite believe her ears. 'Nathan… *café* Nathan? Nathan DaCosta?'

'Of course, Nathan. People round here won't be able to afford it. He's going to push 'em out. For what?' Maude said angrily. 'Gentrification, innit? Or greed.'

'More like highway robbery!' Lila protested. 'It's outrageous. It's not like he probably even needs the money! I can't believe he didn't say anything about it!' She felt betrayed.

'Well, he wouldn't tell you, would he? Lowly employees don't exactly get a say-so in how he runs a different bit o' the business. Not like you're his girlfriend, is it?' Maude gave her a sharp look that said, *At least, I don't think you are, and if something's happened, you better spill it.*

'No… I…' Lila blushed, thinking about the almost-kiss a couple of nights ago. 'I just… I thought we were getting to know each other, that's all. Being friendly. Maybe. I was wrong.'

'Hmm. Well, people like him, they don't make friends with the likes of us.'

'You don't think I'm… seeing him, do you?' Lila gasped. 'I'm not! I wouldn't, Maude. Honestly.'

'That's up to you.' Maude sniffed. 'I heard he's doin' private caterin' now too. Seems he wants me run into the ground every way possible.'

'Oh, Maude.' Lila felt awful. 'I'm sorry, I should have told you, but—'

'You don't owe me anythin', Lila. Yer life's yer own. Free market, innit.'

Lila didn't know what to say. 'I'm sorry, Maude,' she repeated. 'Isn't there anything I can do? About the rent?'

'I doubt it, unless you can persuade Nathan he's in the wrong. But from 'is point of view, I suppose he don't think he is. If you just think about the money, it makes sense. But this kind o' thing's got a personal cost. Couldn't 'ave come at a worse time, either.' Maude looked suddenly shy. 'I'm pregnant. Ten weeks, so I probably shouldn't say, like, but there it is.'

'Pregnant?' Lila repeated, stupidly. A knot of tears clutched her throat.

'Yeah. We weren't tryin', me bein' over forty, but we also weren't *not* tryin', if you know what I mean?' Maude lowered her voice, although they were the only ones in the bakery. 'Due November.'

'Wow.' Lila was lost for words. 'Congratulations,' she made herself say. 'Are you okay? You feel all right?' She coughed, the sudden grief of her own loss like a lump in the throat.

'Feel like death warmed up, truth be told.' Maude sat down on a stool she'd placed behind the counter. 'Probably my age. It's all right, though. Benefit of bein' yer own boss is you can be sick in the loo when you want and no one minds.'

'Of course.' Lila felt like crying, and knew how inappropriate that was. This was happy news, and Maude was her friend. So why did she feel as though the floor had just opened under her? She made herself smile brightly. 'I'm so happy for you!' she said, loudly, as if she was trying to convince herself too.

'Thanks, maid. Look, I didn't mean to come down so hard on you, earlier. I know it's not yer fault, all this business. You okay? You sound a bit… funny.'

'Thanks. You're right – it wasn't my decision, any of this. I mean, I just work for him. If it makes you feel any better, I think the café'll be out of business in a few months, the way he's running it.' Lila turned to look through the bakery window and onto the high street. 'It's such a shame. That place *was* Serafina, you know? It's like he's clouding her memory.'

''Course I know that. It's his business, not yours. I was just a bit… put out, I s'pose, by what happened. And it's not been a good time, what with the 'ormones and the mornin' sickness. Forgive me?' Maude came around to the front of the counter and opened her arms for a hug, which Lila accepted gladly. It was a huge relief to know Maude didn't hate her: the past few weeks had been awkward.

'I just can't get over this thing about Nathan and the rent. I mean, I wonder how many people this affects? I can't believe he's done it. It's just cruel!' Lila murmured into Maude's soft shoulder, channelling all her emotion into that idea. Like she'd always taught herself, she placed her real emotions about Maude being pregnant – and how it made her feel – in a box and shut the lid down tight. She didn't even know how she *did* feel about it, just that it was bad, and feeling bad at a friend's good news must make her a terrible person.

'It's the way of the world,' Maude lamented. 'Nothin' to be done about it, I s'pose.'

'I suppose,' Lila echoed.

'We'll stay in touch, don't you worry.' Maude's voice was so comforting. 'When I get settled next, you come and stay or summink. Us bakers got to stick together.'

Lila hugged her friend back. 'It's not fair,' she muttered into Maude's shoulder. 'I don't want you to go.'

'I know, lover.' Maude patted Lila's back kindly. 'But we was lucky to have it as good as we did in Magpie Cove for all this time. Nothin' stays the same forever, my ma used to tell me.'

Lila knew Maude was right, but she'd only just found Magpie Cove, and it was the only place she'd ever felt that she belonged. She didn't want it to change.

And she was furious. She knew, logically, that Nathan raising rents wasn't any of her business, just like Maude said. She tried to tell herself that she was only outraged on behalf of her fellow residents – and she was, she didn't want Maude's Fine Buns to have to close. She didn't want to lose her friend.

But she also didn't know if she could watch Maude bloom and blossom, in a loving relationship with her husband Simon, when she, Lila, had possibly lost the only chance she'd ever have to have a child. And she hated how mean-spirited that was: she didn't want to believe that about herself. But here it was, a dark thought, an ugly feeling that sat in her throat like a toad and refused to move.

She also knew there was still something between her and Nathan: when she'd been at work on Saturday, after he'd tried to kiss her that night after the pub, there had been an awkward energy between them and he'd hardly said anything to her, coming in for a couple of hours to help with lunch and then beetling off as soon as he could afterwards. Had she wanted something to happen with him? She didn't know. But, somehow, she felt disappointed that he'd turned out to be exactly the cold-hearted capitalist she thought he was when he'd first arrived in the village.

'I hate Nathan DaCosta.' Lila stepped back from Maude's hug and glared at the café across the street. 'I wish Serafina was still alive. It's like she was the glue holding everything together.'

'I know, maid. Like chalk and cheese, they are. But she left him the business, so she must've known somethin' we don't. Maybe he's got some of her good in him. Maybe he needs Magpie Cove like it needed his mum. Stranger things have happened.'

Lila continued to glare at the café. 'I don't know about that, but I'm going to tell him exactly what I think about this. And that is that it stinks.' She let the anger bubble up inside her: it was cleaner, easier, to focus on this than her other confused feelings.

'You don't want to lose your job, maid!' Maude called after her as Lila stormed out of the bakery and over to the café. 'Don't rock the boat on my account!'

But Lila had already gone. Maude watched as Lila paused before the café door to unlock it and then strode in.

'Someone's in for a right talkin' to,' Maude murmured to herself.

Chapter Sixteen

Lila waited all day for Nathan to show up so that she could confront him about Maude's rent, but he didn't come in. In the afternoon, as Lila was clearing up after the lunch rush, she noticed he'd texted her.

Been detained. Hope you coped okay on your own today. See you tomorrow.

Usually, Nathan appeared for a few hours at least to help out here and there, or do his paperwork at one of the café tables. Lila wondered if he was avoiding her: he'd run away pretty fast on Saturday too. *Avoid me all you like, but you're in a world of pain when you do finally show up,* she thought angrily as she wiped down the counter and washed the sponge out under the tap.

The café phone rang.

'Serafina's,' Lila answered, throwing the sponge into the sink.

A nasal, well-to-do voice answered. 'Oh, hello. You recently catered an afternoon tea for my friend and I'd like to book you for a birthday tea next week.'

'Oh. Hi.' Lila looked around for a pen and paper. 'What's your name, please? I'll have to check availability with the team and come back to you.'

'Oh.' The woman's voice sounded put out. 'Bella Cotillard. Two *l*s. The French spelling,' she continued, airily. 'Oliver knows me. I came to your event at the pub last night. It's a birthday party for my stepdaughter. She'll be eight next Thursday. I've invited thirty friends.'

Thirty, or forty-five? Lila wondered caustically as she made notes on the pad, remembering the previous party and having to cater for extras at the last minute. That woman still hadn't yet paid her invoice, either, as far as Lila was aware. She'd have to call up that housekeeper, Sarah – the one who had made eyes at Nathan. She was welcome to him: they'd probably be blissfully happy together in their designer clothes, rolling around in thousand-count Egyptian cotton sheets spritzed with *eau de cologne*.

'Well, as I say, I can't confirm availability until I've checked with the team,' Lila repeated. 'I can probably let you know by tomorrow, though?'

The woman sniffed haughtily. 'Really? Can't you just ask them now? It's just that I've sent all the invitations already.'

Which is my problem how, exactly? Lila made a face at the phone. If Nathan's private catering plan meant she'd have to put up with these rich prima donnas every week, she wasn't sure she really wanted the job.

'So you were looking for an afternoon tea? A birthday cake, individual cakes? Savouries? What kind of thing?' Lila asked.

The woman listed a number of cakes and pastries that she wanted. Lila took notes and repeated back the order.

'Fine. Leave me your number and I'll let you know tomorrow if we can do it,' she concluded. 'Okay. Right. Bye.'

The bells on the door jangled and Lila glanced up to see Mara enter with her boyfriend Brian and her teenage twins, John and Franny. Mara lived down in the house on the beach, and Nathan had hired her to cover on the days Lila didn't work. She had worked at the café in the past, so she knew her way around and left everything tidy. Lila had asked her why she needed another job now if she wrote children's books, but Mara had laughed and said people thought writers earned so much but it was barely a living wage, even when they were reasonably successful.

Lila put the phone down. Now, she had to call Nathan. What would she say first? Tell him about the catering job, or berate him for being a cold-hearted capitalist? It was a tough call. Or it would be when she made it.

'Hey, Lila. Thought we'd drop in and see if you had any lasagne for a takeaway dinner? No one can be bothered to cook.' Mara grinned as she ushered everyone in. 'How's it going?'

'Hey. Fine thanks. Let me see… I think you're in luck.' Lila checked the fridge and pulled out a half-full lasagne tray. 'D'you want me to portion it up?'

'Thanks, that'd be great.' Mara sat down at one of the stools by the counter. 'We've been up on the cliffs all morning. The kids had their first climbing lesson. I thought it'd be a nice opportunity for me and Brian to have a romantic picnic up there, but if I'm honest, I'm exhausted from the stress of watching my children dangle at the end of ropes over a rock face.'

Lila cut up the lasagne into four pieces and put them in two large takeaway boxes. It was good to have a brief distraction from worrying about Nathan.

'What happened to you last night, by the way? Nathan was expecting you for the party,' Mara added. 'I was fine on my own – I mean, all I was doing was serving warm wine. But he thought you were working too?'

Oh, no. With all the business of organising their fundraising event, she'd completely forgotten that she'd agreed to work the same evening at the art launch at the café.

'Oh my…' Lila swore under her breath. 'Mara, I completely forgot! Oliver and I were doing this fundraising event at the Crown and Feathers. Was Nathan really angry?' Her stomach clenched. The last thing she needed now was Nathan being angry with her.

'Umm, I don't think he was impressed, but he seemed okay. You know Nathan. Bit of a closed book.' Mara shrugged. 'I wouldn't worry. Just apologise when you see him.'

Lila suddenly remembered Nathan's call the night before: she'd been just about to do the show, so she'd ignored it, but he obviously had been calling from the café, wondering where she was.

'Hey, Lila. Put in some slices of that chocolate cake, too, if you don't mind.' Brian, Mara's partner, sat down next to her. 'I think we need the sugar.'

'No problem.' Lila lifted the glass dome from over the multi-layered chocolate ganache gateau and placed it carefully on the counter, then lifted the cake plate down and cut four generous slices from it. It wasn't half as good as Maude's, and Lila could have made a much nicer one too, but Nathan was immovable on using this cheap bakery wholesaler. He didn't think people could tell the difference, but he was definitely wrong. Her stomach was in knots – she'd have to call Nathan and explain…

She looked across the street, spotting the CLOSING sign once more in Maude's window and looked away, feeling worse. 'So, did they enjoy the climb? I saw someone up there on the rocks a few weeks ago. I thought they were going to fall at one point, but they had all the ropes and everything. Stressful to watch.' She made herself chatter on, as if she felt fine, but she felt terrible. Lila had never been good with being in the wrong, and she was definitely in the wrong this time. How could she explain that she'd been in a pub down the street singing songs from *Funny Girl*, dressed in a swan costume, when she was supposed to be working? Oliver might have been able to finesse a story that didn't make them sound like a total idiots, but she wasn't sure she could. Her phone lit up on the counter.

U OK, babes? Call me, we need a catch up

It was Alice.

Call you tonight? she texted back quickly. *At work now.*

She wasn't exactly avoiding Alice, but she sort of had to work up to speaking to her friend – Alice was one of the few people in her life who knew about the miscarriage and about Tim. A stressful feeling clutched at her stomach. But maybe she needed to talk to someone – there was a lot going on and she could do with a friendly ear. Plus, she missed Alice. She missed hearing about Alice's life too.

'Fran loved it. John, I'm not sure.' Brian looked over at the twins who were leafing through a magazine at one of the tables and pointing out things to each other. 'But you wouldn't know what he likes, nowadays. Franny tells you her every thought as they happen, but he's even quieter than he used to be. We've hit the moody teen years.'

'We've all been there,' Lila replied, putting the cake slices in an additional takeaway box. She wondered what it was like – to have that burden of caring. She wondered how it felt to watch your child do something dangerous like cliff climbing, even if it was with a teacher. How could you ever risk losing your child in even the smallest way? How did parents cope with facing that risk every day? She had lost a baby. If she ever had a child, would she ever be able to let go enough to let it experience life for itself?

It was a pointless thought. She might not ever *have* a child. She might not be able to. And it wasn't like she even had a boyfriend. She pushed the familiar grief back in its box and slammed the lid down tight. Now wasn't the time to think about that. She had enough to worry about.

She changed the subject and nodded at Maude's window. 'Have you seen the sign over there?'

'I know! We were just talking about it.' Mara shook her head. 'Why would Maude leave? She's doing so well. Have you spoken to her?'

'Her rent's gone up too much. She can't afford it.' Lila raised her eyebrow. 'And guess who her new landlord is.'

Mara frowned. 'Who?'

'Nathan.'

'What, *this* Nathan?' Mara drew a circle in the air with her finger to indicate the café.

'Uh-huh.' Lila explained about Serafina secretly owning a lot of the homes and business property in Magpie Cove. Mara's eyebrows showed her surprise. Brian shook his head.

'I knew her a long time and I had no idea,' he confessed. 'Though it doesn't surprise me. That's the kind of person she was.'

'She did tell me once about her parents leaving her quite a lot of money,' Mara said. 'I mean, I thought she meant enough to buy the café. Not enough to buy the whole village.'

'You never know what's happening in people's lives,' Brian said. 'So, Nathan's pretty rich now. A good catch for someone.' He raised his eyebrow at Lila, who blushed angrily.

'No! I've been thinking about what to say to him all day. It's disgusting behaviour,' she replied testily. 'I'm no more interested in Nathan DaCosta than I am in the Shipwreck and Smuggling Museum's cuttlefish collection. In fact, I'd rather spend time with the cuttlefish than I would him. At least they're not devious and cruel.'

'It does seem rather short-sighted.' Mara frowned. 'But perhaps he has his reasons? I don't know.'

'What reasons could there be? From what Maude said, Serafina owned a lot of flats and houses in the village. What if there are families that have nowhere else to go?'

As soon as she'd said it, Lila thought of Cyd and Betty. What if their house was one of Serafina's?

'It's a difficult one, for sure,' Mara said. 'I'm glad we've got the beach house. Renting can be so insecure. Do you rent? You're not included in this, are you?'

Lila shook her head. 'I don't think so. It's managed by a property management company up in Exeter. I'm concerned for the people who didn't see this coming, though. It's not fair!'

'No, it's not. So, are you going to talk to Nathan about it?' Mara looked at Lila curiously. 'Be careful if you do. I don't know him too well, but he seems kind of closed off. It's hard to know how people like that will react. I mean, you don't want to lose your job.'

'I know.' Lila took a deep breath. 'But I do have to say something.'

'Let me know how you get on.' Mara paid for the food and put it in her tote bag. 'But you might want to lead with an apology for yesterday first. Thanks for the dinner, anyway. I better get this lot home before someone faints from hunger.'

'See you later.' Lila watched them go, then sat down at the counter and stared at Maude's bakery across the street. There must be something she could do. But what?

Chapter Seventeen

Lila's tummy clenched as Nathan walked in that Wednesday morning. She still hadn't quite decided what she wanted to say to him about the rent situation. She'd spoken to him on the phone to organise the birthday tea party for the next day – she and Oliver had done some late-night baking to get everything sorted in time – but that was all business, apart from the part of the conversation where she'd had to apologise for Sunday night. He hadn't said much, just sounded rather disappointed that she hadn't turned up.

'Morning.' Nathan gave her a cautious smile and hung his suit jacket up on the coat hook. It was almost June and was a beautiful day out already. Lila had no idea why he insisted on wearing a suit every day: he could have worn jeans and a T-shirt to work in the café. Some habits were hard to break, she supposed.

'Morning.' Lila continued buttering bread for the selection of sandwiches she made every day: some people still wanted lunch to eat in, but Nathan was keen that they promote takeaway lunches as much as possible. *Saves on the overheads*, he'd explained. Lila hadn't replied that it also depleted the cheery atmosphere of the café.

Since Nathan's changes had been in place, they'd also started getting negative reviews online. Not that they'd ever had much of a social media presence when Serafina was in charge, but Nathan had set up accounts for the café on all manner of platforms and had encouraged Mara and Lila to tweet pictures of cakes for sale, remind people of opening hours and takeaway business, that kind of thing. Lila had tried, but it was tricky when you were busy and holding the fort on your own – which she was most of the time.

Along with the social media accounts, Nathan had entered the café on various local review websites, hoping to cash in on Serafina's reputation as a cosy, homely café with great food and a welcoming atmosphere. He'd put up signs at the counter and around the café that said ENJOYED YOUR MEAL? LEAVE US A REVIEW in capitals, like commands rather than friendly requests. Lila really wanted to at least draw smiley faces on them to make them less threatening, but whenever she thought of it, she either couldn't find a pen or the phone rang or a customer came in.

'Another negative review on cornwallcafés.com.' Nathan showed her his phone screen gloomily. 'Said we were unwelcoming and there was no atmosphere.'

On one hand, she felt bad about not turning up on Sunday, but on the other, she was still cross with Nathan, and his lack of self-awareness about what he was doing to the café – and to the village. She looked up from his phone and searched his face, but it was blank. Could he really have no understanding of the results of his actions? Lila stopped the buttering and wiped her hands on her apron.

'Are you surprised? Look at your signs. LEAVE US A REVIEW. Or you'll be taken out the back and shot, presumably? People don't like having time limits for their coffee, either. And they certainly don't like getting half the size of sandwich for twice the price. You don't even like me playing reggae. We used to have it on all the time.'

'It's not professional,' Nathan snapped. 'And London restaurants give people time limits for dinner all the time. It's normal practice. Cornwall's just stuck in its own little old-fashioned bubble. It needs to catch up with the twenty-first century.'

'Oh, I see. Cornwall's some kind of backward relic, is it?' she replied angrily.

'I can't say I've heard many particularly progressive opinions whilst I've been back.' Nathan fixed her with a stare. 'It hasn't changed much since I was a kid, and I hated it then.'

'Well, maybe the twenty-first century hasn't got so much going for it. Or London, come to that.' Lila stood with her hands on her hips. 'Magpie Cove's the best place I've ever lived: London was an awful place to be. And, if you hadn't noticed, Serafina's isn't a London restaurant. It's a cosy café that everyone used to love until you came along and sucked all the fun out of it. You want good reviews? Go back to the way we used to run things.'

'Wow. Say what you really think, why don't you?' Nathan stared at her unpleasantly. 'Still, at least you turned up for work today. I suppose I should be grateful you're not off in some nightclub in your underwear, doing Diana Ross covers.'

It was a slap in the face, and she knew she had it coming, but it still stung.

'I've apologised for that.' She stood her ground. 'And it wasn't Diana Ross, if you must know. It was Barbra Streisand.'

'Oh, I stand corrected,' Nathan replied sarcastically.

'Yes. You do. And if I were you, I wouldn't be standing there, acting all high and mighty, after what you've done!' she spat. She'd lost her temper now and she didn't care if she lost her job: Nathan Da Costa needed to be told, and if she was the one who had to tell him, then that was just fine.

'Oh. Pray tell. What am I acting high and mighty about?' he shot back.

'I know that you put Maude's rent up on the bakery.' Lila realised that she had raised her voice, but she didn't care. There were no customers anyway. 'How many other properties have you done that to? You know she has to close down now? She can't afford what you're asking.'

'That's not my problem. The rent hadn't been put up in fifteen years.' Nathan narrowed his eyes. 'I've just put the rent levels up to local averages. There's so much maintenance to be done to those properties – they haven't been touched in all that time. Mum may have thought she was doing the community a favour, but some of those flats and shops are a serious risk because she didn't want to hurt people's feelings. I'd rather hurt their feelings than have them die in a fire.'

'It's not a question of hurt feelings. That shop is Maude's livelihood. And we'll be losing a great small business on the high street. It's not like we have that many. Who goes next? Magpie Cove'll become a ghost town.'

'Don't be ridiculous. The high street will attract more boutique small businesses. This is an opportunity to develop Magpie Cove into a premier tourist destination,' Nathan replied crisply.

'Well, what if we don't want it to be a premier tourist destination? What if we like it exactly how it is?' Lila shouted.

'Who's this *we* you're talking about?' Nathan shot back. 'You've been here less than a year. What would you know? You're here for the cheap rent and as soon as you finish your course, you'll be out of here just like everyone else who wants to make something of their lives.'

'You don't know that,' Lila countered. 'You don't know anything about me!' How could she tell him that Magpie Cove had given Lila her life back? That it was the first place in years where she felt she belonged? That walking up on the cliffs had helped her to start to process losing her baby? She had left a broken relationship and a lack of purpose in London, and found friends, community and her passion in Cornwall. 'I love Magpie Cove. It changed my life.'

'Well, I'm happy for you. But while you're baking pastries and singing in pubs, I'm trying to de-tangle my mother's affairs, and it's quite complicated. So I'd appreciate it if you could keep your nose out and focus on the things you're good at.'

Lila stepped back from the counter. 'Oh, like making sandwiches? I should just shut up and let the big man do the important stuff?'

'Since you asked, yes. That *is* what I'm paying you for. When you turn up, that is.'

There was a brief silence: Lila couldn't think of any way to respond, but he'd hurt her feelings and she felt tears welling up in her eyes. She wiped them away furiously – there was no way she would let him see her cry. Nathan took a deep breath and looked as though he wanted to say something more. 'Lila, I didn't mean—'

'Sorry, too busy stacking the dishwasher.' She turned her back on him angrily and started shoving dirty plates into the machine. 'Got to earn my keep.' She was so furious that she didn't turn around until all the dishes were in and she'd set it on to wash, by which time Nathan had taken his suit jacket and left.

Good riddance, Lila thought, still angry. How dare he speak to her like that?

It was mid-afternoon when the gang of teenage boys burst into the café. There was a young mum with her two pre-schoolers at one table, and two women surfers at another table, drinking coffee and talking – their boards leaned against the wall next to the table and they wore shorts and T shirts, their damp hair in plaits.

Lila looked up cautiously when she heard the boys come in. There were a fair number of teens in the village and she knew most of them; the café was popular with young people on a weekend and apart from the odd dramatic break-up or sudden argument, they were well-behaved kids who drank coffee and chatted, appreciating having somewhere to go apart from the beach. There wasn't a high school in Magpie Cove, so they all had to go to Helston by bus and back every day which meant Lila didn't usually see them in the café on a weekday, unless it was the holidays.

However, as soon as the boys entered the café, Lila's sixth sense knew they were going to be trouble. First, they were talking loudly and pushing each other around, and as one of them shoved past the young mums' table, his elbow caught her back. She turned round and called out, but he ignored her and didn't apologise. They approached the counter and milled around, picking up cutlery from the jars of clean knives and forks, jabbing them at each other and dropping them on the counter.

'Can you put those back, please?' Lila raised her voice. One of the boys, already holding two forks, licked both of them and slotted them back in the jar.

'Sorry,' he said, obviously not sorry at all. Lila reached for the jar and took out what she hoped were the same two forks.

'Are you ordering anything, or have you just come in to lick the cutlery?' she asked, tersely. She was also aware that she was on her own in the café, and there were five of these kids. They ranged in age – the youngest looked about thirteen, but a couple were older, maybe sixteen or seventeen, and approaching six feet tall. She wasn't scared of them, but if she needed to hustle them out of the café, it would be a task on her own.

'You got chips?' the tallest one shouted from the back.

'Yes.'

'Five chips to take away, then.'

'All right.' Lila held out her hand, trying not to show relief that they'd ordered the chips to go. 'That's seven pounds fifty, please.'

'I aint got that,' the same boy sneered. 'John can pay. Johnny, pay the nice lady seven fifty of your pocket money.'

The youngest boy scowled, but reached into his pocket and brought out a £10 note and handed it to Lila. She recognised him: Mara's son, one of the twins.

'John, shouldn't you be in school?' she asked, taking the money. Today was Wednesday and it wasn't a holiday as far as she knew. 'Does your mum know you're here?' She looked around at the boys. Come to think of it, she hadn't seen them in the café before.

'Inset day,' John mumbled, taking his change.

'Ooh, does your *mum* know you're here?' echoed one of the other boys. John's expression was thunderous, but he didn't reply. Lila couldn't work out what he was doing with this lot. John was a sweet boy from what she knew of him, which, admittedly, wasn't much. Franny was the talker of the two: Lila felt like she knew quite a lot about Franny, all in all.

'There are other customers here. Can you please behave yourselves?' she asked icily. John had the good grace to look ashamed, but the others obviously didn't care in the slightest. She didn't think they were from Magpie Cove, but if John knew them from school they could be from anywhere up the coast.

'Cheer up, love. Want me to come round there and help out?' the tallest one leered. Lila stepped backwards instinctively but held her nerve. If this kid thought he could intimidate her, he was wrong. She noticed that most of them were quite well-spoken, in fact, and wore branded hoodies and trainers. Rich kids, then, out to cause trouble for some reason.

Lila narrowed her eyes at them. She'd have been mortified if any child of hers disrespected an adult – a stranger, at that – in the way that they were doing right now.

'No, thank you,' she said, instead, shovelling chips into five paper bags and shaking salt onto them. She handed them over the counter and stood with her hands on her hips.

'Anything else?' she said in a tone that inferred that she really hoped not.

'John, you going to buy us anything else?' One of the others sat on a nearby table and rested his shoes on one of the chairs. 'I fancy a slice of cake.'

'Can you get off that table, please. People have to sit there,' Lila raised her voice.

'Make me,' the boy said, pushing sandy hair out of his eyes. Lila bit her lip: she was so tempted to grab him by his ear and hoist him off the table, the rude little beggar. Where had he picked up such an arrogant attitude?

The two female surfers were waiting to pay their bill and were standing behind the teens, trying to get past.

'Excuse me,' one of them said, pointedly.

'Keep your knickers on, Baywatch,' the tallest boy called out.

'What did you just say?' The other surfer pushed the kid in front of her so that he moved away: like most who surfed regularly, she was fit and strong. Lila estimated she could probably make mincemeat of a teenage boy.

'Nothing.' The kid looked away.

'Oh really? I thought you just insulted my friend,' the woman replied.

'Never said nothing,' the boy muttered.

'Learn some bloody manners.' The woman looked him up and down, and paid the bill.

'I'm so sorry about them,' Lila apologised.

'It's not your fault, love.' The surfer shrugged. Lila thought that maybe she and her friend wouldn't come back to the café next time, though. This was a bad review that was nothing to do with Nathan's efficiency measures, for once.

'Right. I think you've made enough trouble, so I'd like you all to leave now.' Lila crossed her arms over her chest and stared at the gang. 'And you're not welcome in here again. Okay?'

'You can't throw us out. We've got rights,' one of the boys called out.

'Yeah. You're, like, damaging our human rights.' The oldest one laughed.

'Take it to the high court, then. I don't care. Leave, or I call the police,' she threatened, though they probably knew as well as she did that there were three police officers in Magpie Cove and they were all part-time.

'Ooh, testy,' the ringleader cooed. He leaned over the counter. 'What're you going to do? Beat me with your rolling pin?'

'Is there a problem here?'

Lila looked up to see Nathan in the doorway. Even though she was still cross with him from earlier, she was relieved to see him. She would have been relieved to see any other adult that could help her in that moment: the lone mum in the corner with the two little ones wasn't exactly free to leap into action.

'It looks like you're bothering my staff member. Is that what's happening here?' Nathan continued walking up to the gang.

'Not doing anything.' The ringleader put his hands in his pockets and glared at Nathan.

'Oh, that's good. Then you won't mind leaving. Now.' Nathan stepped close so that his face was just a few inches away from the kid's. 'We have a staff meeting.'

The kid stared at Nathan for a few seconds – Nathan was taller and much more heavily built, being twenty years older and pretty muscular, Lila reminded herself – and obviously realised that he'd lose any fight that might follow.

'We're just going.' He loped off, holding his chips. 'Come on, then,' he called over his shoulder to his gang. Lila watched with concern as John followed them.

'You all right?' Nathan asked when they'd left.

'Fine. I was dealing with it,' Lila snapped. She was glad he'd appeared when he did, but she didn't want to give Nathan another reason to think of her as the little woman. He'd already made his views on that subject perfectly clear.

'I know. Sometimes boys that age only respond to bigger boys, though.' He tutted, picking up some stray chips from the floor. 'You seen them before?'

'No. Well, I recognise one of them. He's Mara son, in fact. John.' Lila frowned. 'I doubt she'd be happy if she knew he was running around with them. They said they had an inset day, but they might well have been lying.'

'Oh. We should tell her.' Nathan walked back to the front of the café and looked out of the door onto the street. 'I haven't met her kids before. They've gone. Looked like they were just out to cause trouble.'

'Yeah,' Lila agreed. 'They weren't the kids we usually get in here. They must be from his school. Kids from all over go there.'

'Look. I came back to say sorry about earlier. I said things I didn't mean.' Nathan took a disinfectant spray and squirted the table that the boy had sat on, and the chair where he'd rested his feet. 'It wasn't fair.'

'I guess the rent thing isn't any of my business,' Lila said, although she didn't actually believe that, particularly. 'But I appreciate you saying sorry.'

'Okay.' Nathan wiped the table and the chairs and put the cleaning materials on the counter. 'Friends, then? I'd rather you didn't hate me. It would make working life quite difficult.' He reached for her hand and squeezed it.

'I don't hate you,' she murmured, even though she really *had* when she'd said it to Maude earlier that morning. It was so strange when he touched her: it was like she was suddenly ultra-aware of his skin on hers, as if all the rest of her surroundings faded out of focus. It was impossible to hold hate in her mind when it happened.

'Good,' he breathed, not moving his hand away. He was giving her an intense look she didn't want to break. 'Because I don't hate you. In fact, I... I like you. A lot.'

He leaned forward. She found herself learning forward slightly too. *He's going to kiss me,* she thought. *What the hell is happening? This morning we were shouting at each other.*

Suddenly, she remembered what he'd said earlier. Yes, there was some kind of weird chemistry between her and Nathan DaCosta, but did she really want to kiss a man who had all but told her he thought her only good for making sandwiches – and that she should leave all the clever stuff to him? That wasn't who Lila was.

She stood up straight and released her hand from his.

'I should get on,' she said, and walked into the back room. She took some grounding breaths and shook her head. There was no way that Nathan was going to make her forget who she was – or who he had proved himself to be. Chemistry was one thing, but doing the right thing was quite another.

Chapter Eighteen

Lila stared at the official letter in her hands. She read it again, to be sure she'd got it right. Unfortunately, she had.

Her rent was being raised from the beginning of the next month – and it wasn't a small rise, either. She looked up, through the window over the door frame, at the blue Cornish sky. There was no way she could afford this.

The letterhead was from a solicitor based in Exeter, but it gave the name of the property management company: Lila traced her finger over it on the paper. Polished Properties Ltd. She remembered it now, from signing the original contract. It had all been done by post; Serafina had arranged it for her. Could she possibly have been Lila's landlady as well as Maude's? Maude had told her that quite a few people in Magpie Cove had got sudden news of a rent raise from Nathan – it seemed like too much of a coincidence that now she had, too.

And how had Serafina just happened to know about a flat in Magpie Cove that had needed a tenant – with a low rent that was perfectly pitched to suit Lila's part-time working at the café? Something nagged at Lila's memory: Serafina had told her once what her surname meant in English. Lila got out her phone and tapped 'Lucido' into a translation website. In English, 'Lucido' meant polished or shiny. Polished Properties.

So, it had been her all along.

Lila felt tears spring to her eyes. It was another kindness that Serafina had bestowed on her, and she hadn't even known. Now, it was too late to thank her.

Lila walked back into the kitchen holding her post and put it on the table; she picked up her mug of tea and drank it, staring out of the large back window onto the gardens beneath.

This meant that Nathan was now her boss and her landlord – and Nathan had chosen to make it impossible for her to stay in Magpie Cove. Why had he done it? It was bad enough that he'd decided to raise the rents of the people he didn't know in the village – who, like Maude, also couldn't afford to stay. But Lila felt personally affronted that Nathan hadn't even had the decency to tell her about it, considering that she saw him every week. When had he decided to do it? When he sat with her by Cyd's hospital bed? When he helped her carry scones and cakes into a room full of middle-aged rich women? After he'd tried to kiss her in the café?

Lila would be forced to move and she'd have to hope she could get another job until she finished her course. After that, she'd have to move back in with Aunt Joan until another option came along. Her heart twisted. She loved Magpie Cove so much. She really didn't want to leave. And if she did, what would happen to Cyd and Betty? Who would look after them?

She looked at the kitchen clock. She'd have to get going – it was a college day and she hadn't put her rollers in yet or ironed the full 50s-style skirt she'd pulled out of her wardrobe for the day. But her heart was heavy and, an hour later, as she drove along the winding Cornish road from Magpie Cove to St Ives, even the sun through the open window and the sparkling coastline that ran alongside the road did nothing to improve her mood.

Later, after class, Lila sat with a takeaway coffee on the steps of the college and people watched. The college sat near to the centre of town and was surrounded by boutiques, bakeries and cafés. It was beautiful – the college architecture was old and stately, full of stone curlicues and flourishes. The old grey stone buildings that housed the shops around it showed carefully restored stonemasonry advertising the businesses they used to be: Archer's Fine Tobacco, Tea Rooms, Dressmaker. Nowadays, the residential property above those shops went for high prices, even to rent. Lila tapped through the results that she'd found on a local rentals app: she definitely couldn't afford to live on her own in St Ives, even if she picked up another part-time job. She'd have to work more hours around her course: maybe if she found a night job as well, that would help.

'Penny for them, gorgeous.' Oliver sat down on the steps and nudged her. 'You were quiet in class today. Cat got your tongue?'

'Nope. Evil landlord got greedy.' Lila passed him the letter, which she had open on her lap. 'It's not just me. Maude got hers raised too, and loads of people in Magpie Cove. You won't believe the worst of it, either.'

'What's the worst? Wow, this is a lot more, huh?' Oliver scanned the letter and gave it back to her.

'The *worst* is that my new landlord is actually Nathan.' Lila drank the last of her coffee.

'Hot Nathan? No way!'

'Afraid so. It seems that Serafina owned a lot of property around town. He inherited all of it and he's apparently decided to gentrify the village.'

'Wow. I did not see that coming.' Oliver sucked air through his teeth.

'Me neither. Oh, by the way. We've got a catering job next Thursday if you can make it. Another Real Housewives of St Ives party. Which I'll have to smile through even though I can't stand the sight of my boss…'

'I'll come prepared for an atmosphere, then. Kind of tight turnaround again, but I can probably do it. I could do with the money.' Oliver raised his eyebrow. 'I just got Juliet serviced and the poor thing needs new tyres and some new flippety widget I've forgotten the name of.'

'I still think it's weird you call your car Juliet.' Lila watched a mother with a buggy walk serenely past the row of shops at the other side of the square. A twinge of grief pulled in her stomach.

'Why not? It's a very sophisticated name. And Juliet Stevenson is one of our finest British actresses.' Oliver sniffed. 'Her performance in *Truly, Madly, Deeply* is completely underrated.'

'I don't know that it is particularly underrated. I think that film got quite a good critical reception. It won a BAFTA.'

'Well, it doesn't get talked about enough,' Oliver huffed.

'It came out in 1992. The world's moved on.' Lila squeezed her friend's hand.

'Hmm. We never really talked that much about how your conversation with Nathan went – about him supporting our fundraising. Other than he didn't go for it.' Oliver put on a pair of designer sunglasses.

'He said we needed a business plan and then maybe he'd help us. Not that I'd ever accept his money now.' Lila blushed involuntarily, thinking of what had happened afterwards. The almost-kiss.

'Oh.' Oliver peered at Lila and lifted her own sunglasses off her face. 'Why are you blushing? Did something happen between you?'

'No! Of course not,' Lila lied and grabbed her sunglasses back. 'Anyway, what's the point in a supper club if I have to move out of the village? I won't be there to run it.'

'Something did happen. I can tell!' Oliver crowed. 'Tell me, otherwise I'll make a huge scene and embarrass you. You know I can.'

'No.' Lila hugged her arms around her. 'I'm not telling you.'

Oliver stood up on the steps and started singing a song from *Grease*.

'Oli! Sit down!' Lila hissed.

Oliver sang loudly, one hand pressed to his heart and one held out in supplication to the other students.

'Oh, FINE!' She pulled his hand so that he sat down.

He grinned expectantly. 'Spill it. Or I do "Look at Me, I'm Sandra Dee". Or my Juliet Stevenson in tears. People will think you've injured me.'

Lila glared at him. 'He almost kissed me. Very briefly. But then he stopped and acted like it was all a massive mistake, which it was, now that I know he's a horrible, greedy little man with no moral compass.'

'What was it like? Be honest.' Oliver leaned forward. 'You might not like him very much, but the sex could still be fantastic. Remember when I had that thing with Mark Bullock? Boringest man in the history of the world. Amazing in bed.'

'Mark Bullock wasn't the most boring man in the history of the world. He just wasn't into musicals,' Lila corrected him.

'He was a football fan,' Oli added. 'I shudder whenever I think about it. What could have been…'

'Millions of very nice men like football,' Lila argued. 'Anyway, I feel like we're getting off the point here. The point is that Nathan DaCosta is *not* a very nice man.'

'Hot,' Oli breathed. 'He's a bad man. He could evaluate my stock portfolio any night of the week. Who wants a nice man anyway?'

'I do!' Lila cried. 'I just want someone who isn't prepared to evict old ladies from their houses onto the street. Is that too much to ask? Oh, and not act like kissing me is like…' she searched for a comparison.

'Frenching an otter in lipstick?'

'Thanks.' Lila rolled her eyes.

'Hmm. So you can't afford the new rent?'

'No way. I'll have to move and get a new job. Maybe work nights too until the end of the course. I'm sure I can make it work… it just means disaster management for a few months. No time for other stuff.'

'I mean, you could stay with me, hon, but there's barely enough room to swing a cat.' Oliver put his arm around her shoulders. 'Have you looked at rentals? I can help you.'

'I know, and thanks. I mean, I can share a student house if I have to. There are a few of those at the edge of town I could afford. It's just that it makes it more difficult to get any practice baking in a shared kitchen. At least when you live on your own you can spend hours doing it and you're not in anyone's way. Plus, the kitchen in my flat's really good. It's got space for my mixers, all my tins, the oven's good. You know.'

'I know.' Oliver squeezed her shoulders. 'I wouldn't want to have to practice bake in a kitchen with three students. You'd be forever picking alphabetti spaghetti out of your banana chiffon pie. Most of these –' he inclined his head to the groups of students sunning themselves on the steps – 'they're either proper grown-ups with their own houses, or rich brats that Daddy pays the rent for.' He sighed. 'I wish I had a rich Daddy. Real or adopted.'

'Me too, I guess.' Lila groaned. 'This is rubbish.'

'Well, when do you have to be out of the flat?' Oliver smiled at an attractive young man walking past.

'Nice voice,' the young man called out.

'You should hear my morning arpeggio,' Oliver shot right back.

'Four weeks' time. Hey. Concentrate, please.' She tapped him on the leg.

'Sorry.' Oliver returned his gaze to her.

'Cyd gets home from hospital this week. I wanted to be ready to support them by the time they were home.'

'Well, best laid plans, and all that.' Oliver shrugged. 'Can't be helped.'

'When I find a new place, I'll know more about what I can and can't do. Is that fair?' Lila laid her head on Oliver's shoulder.

'Of course it's fair, missus. It's not like the people who gave us money are expecting a quarterly report, they just had a good night out and wanted to help the oldies.' Oliver reasoned. 'For now, let's make Cyd and Betty a nice dinner next week? Then see what you can manage after that, when you get settled. We've got the money in the bank, and we can make a few bits here and there. I can take cake around to the others as well, have a chat and a cuppa once a week at the very least while you're sorting yourself out. Then we can start the dinners plan, and then think about fundraising more if we think it's got legs.'

'Okay.' It was annoying that, after Sunday's success, everything had changed so much and so quickly.

'What shall we make them? My famous soufflé? Your not-so-famous one?' Oliver nudged her in the ribs. 'See. There's the smile that I fell in love with.'

'Oli, have a day off.' Lila nudged him back. 'What about a beef stroganoff, wild rice, seasonal greens? We can make some bread and take along some of that salted butter from Gordon's.'

'Ohh, I love that stuff. The salt crystals are to die for.' Oliver moaned theatrically. 'Fine. I think something soft for dessert. What about lemon posset? It travels well. And we can take along some biscuits or cakes in a tin to leave with them. That'll be lovely.'

'It really will.' Lila's heart ached with the knowledge that she'd soon have to leave Magpie Cove and that Cyd and Betty would be further away. She wouldn't be able to just look in on them like she was used to. Caring for Cyd and Betty was connected somehow in her mind to her baby: it made her feel better to care for someone – even if she didn't always care for herself very well.

Chapter Nineteen

'Now, then, what's all this?' Betty leaned on Lila's arm as she guided her into the front room. Cyd was following with Oliver, her eyes scrunched tightly shut.

'No peeking!' Lila chastised Betty, who definitely had her eyes slightly open.

'I'm not! But I don't want to trip on the rug, do I?'

'All right. Open your eyes.' Lila settled Betty in her favourite upright chair, her arms on the wooden armrests. 'Ta-dah!'

'Ooh, bless my soul!' Oliver had helped Cyd into her chair next to Betty and she'd opened her eyes too. 'Candles! What's all this?'

Lila pressed play on her phone, having brought along her digital speaker, and the sound of a lindy hop band segued tastefully into the background.

'Oh, that takes me back!' Betty pointed to a black and white photo in a gilt frame on the wall behind where Lila stood. 'There's me an' Cyd in our dancin' dresses. When we did lindy hop we had these brilliant dresses, didn't we, Cyd? Big skirts an' ruffled underskirts, tight in at the waist. I had yellow with black polka dots an' a white frilly underskirt an' Cyd had a pink dress with pink underskirt. We looked bloody gorgeous! Flat shoes, mind. Can't do all that twirlin' an' flippin' over upside down in heels. We had to wear special knickers as well, so no one saw our unmentionables when we went upside down.' Betty cackled. 'Remember that, Cyd? That was when we danced with Peter an' David. I miss them, I do.'

'Oh, so do I,' Cyd trilled. 'Beautiful dancers they were. An' perfect gentlemen too. Always saw us home. We used to make a four for bridge sometimes too.'

'Must have been nice to spend time together as two couples.' Oliver had gone back into the kitchen, returning with a cushioned tray which he settled on Cyd's lap. 'At least it was something you could share safely together.'

'Well, you say that, my love, but we didn't ever really talk about being gay. I s'pose it was just enough that we knew we both were. We never knew any other lesbians until the mid-80s.' Cyd's eyes widened, looking at the plate on the tray. 'Now, what's this?'

'Beef stroganoff – very tender – seasonal greens, with creamy mashed potatoes. Here's a glass of carrot juice to go with it.' He grinned at Cyd's outraged expression. 'If you drink it all, you can have a sherry after.'

Lila brought out a matching tray for Betty and balanced it carefully on her lap.

'Ooh, it's nice to be home.' Cyd sighed happily. 'What nice young people you are to do all this for us.'

'It's nothing. We're just glad you're okay.' Lila sank into Cyd and Betty's ancient purple sofa next to Oliver. 'Better than hospital food, then?'

'Just a bit.' Betty rolled her eyes. 'They does their best, God love 'em. But I always say, good nutrition's so important in keepin' healthy. Thankfully we's always been healthy eaters, 'ent we, Cyd? When I was a girl, my dad grew most of our fruit 'n' veg in the garden. Big plot, it was. We had apple trees all the way to the fields beyond. Potatoes, my mum used to wrap in newspaper an' keep in boxes under the stairs. We had pears, plums in the summer, greens, broccoli, tomatoes, the lot. We never starved, though there weren't much money around.'

'I'd love to do that,' Lila mused. 'Have a big kitchen garden. Maybe for the café. It could be much more self-sufficient than it is. We buy everything in. We could at least grow the veg.'

'Not exactly how Nathan sees it going, though, is it?' Oliver leaned back on the sofa. 'We've got that private catering do tomorrow. I mean, I enjoyed the last one. I don't mind at all. Not quite your vision, though, is it?'

'Not really. I thought I'd love catering private parties. I enjoy the baking part, but last time…'

'What, maid?' Cyd looked up from her meal. 'Sounded like a hoot and a half to me when Oliver told me.'

'It was all right.' Lila thought about the party. 'I suppose… I didn't like the waste. There was so much left over, and because most of it had cream in it, we had to throw it away. And I didn't like the people, really. They just acted like it was their birthright to be served cakes and champagne. At least in the café, people say please and thank you. And it feels like we're helping the locals. Like when you come in for your breakfasts.'

'Well, I like it. Can't wait to party with another room of tipsy Housewives of St Ives.' Oliver shrugged. 'It's not their fault they're rich. Goodness knows they've got to let off steam somehow.'

'Yes, those poor underprivileged women.' Lila rolled her eyes. 'How must they cope?'

'Come on, Lila. You don't know them. Bad things happen to everyone.' Oliver nudged her in the ribs. 'Even you. Honestly, Betty, this one's seen her share of suffering, don't you think? You can see it in her perfectly made-up eyes. I keep telling her she's our very own Elizabeth Taylor. You should own it, Lila, whatever it is. Like Liz in *Cat on a Hot Tin Roof*.'

'What, confess my sexless marriage to an alcoholic?' Lila raised an eyebrow. 'I don't want to disappoint you, but I haven't done that. Anyway, we're here for our two favourite ladies today. How's your meal?'

'Lovely, ta.' Cyd picked up her carrot juice suspiciously, drank a little and then smiled. 'Ooh. It's quite nice, innit?'

'Well, we thought we could pop around and make you a good, cooked dinner a couple of nights a week, if that was okay with you?' Lila said, exchanging looks with Oliver. 'Oli can do Mondays, and I can do Thursdays. And we can leave a tin of cake and some bread with you every week. We can pop to the shops as well if you need things. Now that you're not as mobile.'

'Ah, that's a lovely offer.' Betty gave a strained smile as she swallowed her mashed potato. 'We'd be ever so grateful to have that while we're still here. But the thing is, we've got to move out. Social services has got us both into the same care home, an' I think they have their own caterin' there. Not as nice as this, o' course. Sorry, my loves. I wish we could stay, but we can't.'

'A care home? Why?' Lila's heart clenched. This was terrible news. Cyd and Betty had only just got home.

'Well, we're not as limber as we was, maid. There's that. Hospital said we shouldn't really be potterin' away in this house on our own no more, what with Cyd's fall an' my health not as good as it was. Plus, our landlord seems to want to put the rent up, an' we can't afford it. We was always rentin' this place, I had a bit o' money put away an' it was cheap. But now, it feels like time to go, an' the care home's nice. We've seen pictures, haven't we, Cyd?' She turned to her partner and gave her a brave grin. 'New adventure for us.'

'But you love this place!' Lila cried out. This was Nathan's doing, again. He seemed to be systematically destroying Magpie Cove, house by house and person by person. First Maude, then her, and now Cyd and Betty? It was unconscionable. 'I can't believe Nathan. This is a step too far. WAY too far!' She stood up and started pacing around the room. 'How dare he evict two elderly women? You can't go into a care home. You can't!' Lila started to cry. Oliver jumped up and put his arms around her.

'Hey, now. Calm down. It's not so bad.' He hugged her and spoke quietly. 'It sounds like this is the right thing, even though it's all happened at the same time as Nathan being an idiot. Don't get me wrong, I'm not disputing the fact that it's horrible to evict pensioners—'

'I can't believe he would do this. Any of it.' Lila wiped her eyes. 'Sorry, ladies. It's just a bit of a shock.'

'Oh, maid. Don't cry.' Betty tried to put her meal aside and get up, but there was nowhere to put the tray. 'Damn this old body! See, I can't even get up to give yer a hug. Don't you worry 'bout us. We'll be together an' we'll be fine, I promise. You can still come an' visit us an' bring all the cakes you like.' She looked around thoughtfully. 'I shall miss the old place, though.'

'So will I,' Cyd agreed. 'But we're just too old, my love. Comes a time when you have to accept help.'

'I suppose so,' Lila admitted. 'Sorry. I'm just so angry with Nathan about all this rent business. I told him exactly what I thought about it. It's just that… I guess I was being naïve. I thought if someone – well, if I – told him he was being cruel, he'd change his mind. He's just a cold hearted, money-grabbing…' she trailed off. 'I thought he was better than this.'

'Well, let's enjoy tonight, anyway.' Oliver went into the kitchen and came back with a sherry bottle and four glasses on a tray. 'I was saving this until after dessert, but I feel like we probably need it now.' He poured four glasses, handed them to Cyd, Betty and Lila and took one himself. 'To new beginnings, and in thanks for friends, good times and good food.'

They clinked their glasses.

'Where's the care home?' Lila asked, trying to sound upbeat and probably failing. For her, a move to St Ives was a minor problem: she was young, she'd find something and get on with her life. But for Cyd and Betty, this move was something else entirely. They must know they'd never live independently again.

'Not far. Off that roundabout on Morven Road.' Betty took Cyd's hand and gave it a squeeze. 'We've got a big room an' bathroom to share, an' hers and hers beds. They've even got those motorised up-and-down backs, what help yer get up of a mornin'. Bloody marvellous, they are. You'll have to visit, Lilly.'

'Just try and stop me.' Lila made herself be positive for Cyd and Betty, but, inside, she was heartbroken. Since he'd arrived, Nathan had destroyed everything she loved in Magpie Cove: the café, her home, now her friends had to move away. She had come to love this little Cornish village with its odd ways and funny characters, but now everything was changing. Why couldn't everything just stay as it was? She'd just started to feel like Magpie Cove was somewhere she could rely on: a secure place in the world where the sand wouldn't constantly shift under her feet. Yet, like everything else in her life, it turned out there was nothing she could hold onto after all.

Chapter Twenty

Lila could hear Oliver screeching with laughter in the dining room of the huge house, but she couldn't even manage to plaster a fake smile on her face. Moodily, she assembled a plate of pastries, piping them with crème patissiere and placing them on a tray. She'd take them in in a minute, but for now she needed some time out.

Nathan hadn't come to help them with this party, which she was grateful for. Today, he'd got Mara to cover at the café so that Lila could do the party with Oliver. But what would she say to him when she eventually saw him again? How could she stand to be in the same room when she hated him this much? Sure, Cyd and Betty had assured her that it was their choice to move to a care home – the letter from the solicitors about the rent had just been the push they needed. Social services had already made the suggestion. But Lila still couldn't get over how anyone could be okay with turfing out two vulnerable women almost in their eighties from the house they'd lived in for decades and not caring where they went.

It had been a bad few days. She'd had her usual nightmare every night, rather than once every week or so, and this time, as well as the baby in the house, she was searching for Cyd and Betty who she knew were lost in the garden somewhere.

She still hadn't found a job or a flat in St Ives and she had less than three weeks to find both. On her way to the party today, she'd posted a formal letter giving her notice about working at the café to Nathan, also informing him that she'd be moving out of the flat at the same time.

Nathan hadn't yet mentioned the flat to her at all. To think that she'd ever been attracted to him. He was clearly one of those sociopathic city boys that had a spreadsheet where their heart should be.

She'd hoped, at first, that she might stay involved with Nathan's private catering thing, but she couldn't very well give in her notice at the café and from the flat but add that she was still available for upscale catering jobs here and there. *I don't want to, anyway,* she thought, listening to the braying laughter reverberating down the hallway. She knew it was unfair to judge these people. They were only having a good time, and it was a kid's birthday party, at that. *I guess I just didn't realise that I didn't want this until I did it,* she thought.

Oliver appeared in the kitchen, grinning.

'Those mums are a hoot! I've just got three more birthday party bookings. Look.' He dropped three business cards onto the kitchen top. 'Adult ones, this time. The kids loved your birthday cake. They've been hustled off by circus performers into the garden now. The grown-ups are drinking champagne in the dining room. I need to take them in some savouries as well as these pastries or they'll throw up,' he regaled Lila merrily. 'Give me a hand with the trays?'

'Sure.' Lila picked up a tray of her speciality vegan sausage rolls and vegetarian sushi and followed Oliver into the dining room.

'Ladies, nibbles are here! This is my colleague Lila, who's responsible for the delicious savouries and the birthday cake.' Oliver set his trays down on a long glass dining table in a room with elaborate silver patterned wallpaper.

'Oh, the cake was amaaaazing,' one of the mums purred. 'Sylvia adored the hidden sweets in the middle. She loves rainbow layer cake and she said yours was the best she's ever had. So, thank you.'

'You're welcome.' Lila smiled. 'Are the children enjoying the party?'

'Oh, they're happy. God knows I've thrown enough money at it, so they should be!' the woman laughed uproariously. 'Gives us a chance for a natter anyway if they're not around.'

'I'll just tidy up a bit,' Lila said in a low voice to Oliver. 'You stay here. Let me know if they want more of anything.'

She started stacking some empty trays and piled up a few used plates. Oliver had perched on the end of the table and was regaling a couple of the mums with some story or another and they were gazing up at him with complete adoration. Lila smiled to herself, despite her terrible mood: he'd really found his niche.

'Of course, it's no wonder John's running with the wrong crowd if that's what's happening at home,' one of the mothers said, near to where Lila was standing. She continued clearing up, half listening.

'I heard Gideon's moved his new girlfriend in. Of course his ex-wife, Mara, is long gone to live in that terrible beach shack or something, but it's quite hard when a parent introduces a new person to the living arrangements,' another woman chipped in. 'It's some woman Gideon met abroad. Not even the same one he left Mara for.'

'No wonder John's rebelling,' another tutted. 'My little Georgie has never got on with his stepmother. Not that I blame him. She's only interested in having her hair done and spending all my ex's money.'

Were they talking about Mara Hughes? Mara lived in a beach house in Magpie Cove and Lila knew she was separated from her husband. Brian was her partner, and the kids lived with them, though Lila thought they still stayed with their dad now and then.

'That group of boys. No discipline at home,' the first woman tutted. 'You wouldn't see my kids running wild like that. I heard they've been bullying other kids. Taking their money. It's all on social media too these days,' she added. 'The bullying, that is. They can't ever get away from it. A shame, really.'

'I always thought that Mara was a bit stuck-up,' sniffed the other woman. 'Thought she was too good for us, though I don't know why. Maybe John's picked that up from her?'

Lila was positive now that they were talking about Mara Hughes: these women's kids obviously went to the same school as Franny and John in St Ives. John had been on her mind since he'd come into the café with those other boys who had behaved so badly. Yes, he'd been with them, but they hadn't exactly been friendly to him. She hoped he was okay. She hadn't had the chance to talk to Mara about it yet – it felt like something she wanted to tell Mara in person rather than on the phone, and they hadn't had seen each other since the day the boys had come into the café. Lila imagined that she'd certainly want to know if her son was being gossiped about.

She took the plates into the kitchen and checked her phone. There was a message from Maude.

Haven't seen you for a while – hope you're not avoiding the bakery? Having a baby shower and would love you to come.

Lila stared at the message. She didn't want to go, that was the truth of it. Ever since Maude had told her she was pregnant, she *had* been avoiding the bakery. She was glad for Maude – she really was. But talking about babies was hard for her. Maude was someone that she could have talked to about the miscarriage, but now that she was pregnant, it felt like bad luck to mention it. Maude wouldn't want to hear about what happened to Lila. Quite honestly, the way she was at the moment, Lila didn't trust herself to go to the party, but she also knew it would look awful if she said no.

You'll just have to manage, she told herself. *It's an hour or two of your life, and that's all. Just pull yourself together.*

Without giving herself a chance to chicken out, Lila tapped out a brief message in reply to Maude and sent it.

Can't wait – let me know the details.

She set her phone down and felt tears welling up in her throat. *You're just tired,* she reasoned with herself. *A few nights' broken sleep makes everyone a bit touchy. Just try and power through.* She knew she had to call Alice, too – her friend had left two messages on her answerphone – but she really didn't know what to say. When she felt like this, Lila tended to batten down the hatches and shut everyone out, and that was exactly what she wanted to do now.

Chapter Twenty-One

Lila had just got home from college and made herself a cup of tea when there was a knock at the door. She'd planned to head down to the beach with a picnic as the evenings were so light at the moment, and she'd arranged to call Alice too.

'Oh. It's you.' She realised that her tone didn't sound that friendly, but she wasn't well disposed towards Nathan DaCosta just now. 'Sorry, I'm going out in a minute, so it'll have to be quick.'

'I got your letter.' Nathan held the envelope she'd posted yesterday morning in his hand. 'You're giving your notice?'

'Two weeks. It's what's in my contract.' Lila folded her hands over her chest.

'I really don't want you to leave,' he replied. His manner was his usual businesslike one, and it riled her.

'Tell your face,' she retorted.

'What?'

'I mean, if you don't want me to leave, then at least show some emotion. But then, you can't, can you? You're cold, through and through.'

'That's… you're being unfair.' He looked away, down the street. 'Can't I come in and talk about this?'

'Not really, no. I'm going out soon. Look, I can't afford to live in Magpie Cove anymore, so I can't work at the café. It's very simple. And, quite frankly, even if I didn't have to move out of the village, I still wouldn't want to work for you, after what you've done.'

Nathan looked confused.

'What have I done?' he asked. 'Is this about Maude again?'

'No, it's not about Maude!' Lila yelled. 'Well, yes, it is, in fact. It's about all of us. Maude, me, Cyd and Betty, goodness knows how many more of us you're putting on the street!'

'You and Cyd and Betty?' He frowned again. 'I don't understand.'

'Oh, he doesn't *understand*,' Lila told the air. 'Look,' she rummaged in the paperwork on the table by the door and thrust her letter from his solicitor in his face, 'that clear enough for you?'

Nathan took the letter and read it.

'Oh…' He looked taken aback. 'Lila, I didn't realise… I'm sorry… let me explain.'

'You don't have anything to explain. It's all there in black and white,' Lila fumed. 'Now, I can move to St Ives and get a job there. I'm young, I can cope. But what really gets me is that you've done the same to two elderly women who now have to go into a *care home* because you're pulling the rug out from under them!' she yelled. 'Do you know what hardships Cyd and Betty have gone through? And now this? It's an insult. It's inhuman.' She glared at him.

Nathan bit his lip.

'Look, if you'd just listen…' he ventured.

'I will not listen, thank you. I'll work my two weeks' notice and that's all you'll get from me,' she snapped. 'If you want staff for any more private parties then ask Oliver, but I'm not interested in that either. All I can say is that your mother would be spinning in her grave if she knew what you've done. I hope you're proud of yourself,' she yelled, and slammed the door in his face.

Lila stood behind the door, sobbing. She knew Nathan was still standing out there: she hadn't heard him leave.

'Lila?' He knocked gently at the door. 'Lila, please let me explain.'

'Go away. I don't want to talk to you,' she shouted through her tears. 'Please.'

There was a silence, then she heard his footsteps leading away from the door. Lila sat at the bottom of the stairs and sobbed.

Everything had gone wrong since Serafina had died. Magpie Cove had been Lila's sanctuary and now she was being forced out of it. She didn't want to go back to her old life – though, rationally, she knew that her life had changed now and would never change back, even if she didn't live in Magpie Cove. She wasn't the same person who had put up with a job she hated and a relationship that was dead in the water. But she didn't want to leave Magpie Cove, nonetheless.

Living and working in St Ives could be just as restorative, she reasoned with herself. She was being silly. Perhaps it was just the thought of more upheaval that was making her anxious: having to move, having to find a new job. St Ives wasn't exactly the other side of the world.

But perhaps it was more that. Since the miscarriage and the move away from London, she felt so much less equipped to deal with stressful situations. Before the miscarriage, she coped daily with a job she hated, Tim's complaints and a stressful commute where she'd more likely than not be shoved up against some stranger's armpit for forty minutes twice a day. She hadn't thought anything of it at the time – or been aware that she had. Now, her tolerance for stress felt lower than it ever had.

But maybe, she thought as she sat on the stairs, looking at the evening sun streaming through the window above the door, *maybe it's just that your ability to pretend has gone. It's not that life feels more stressful – it's that you're happier. And so when something bad happens, it's exceptional rather than part of the terrible norm.*

Lila put her head in her hands and took some deep breaths. *It's going to be okay*, she told herself. *You'll get through the rest of your course, you'll find somewhere to live, and then a new phase of your life can start. You don't know what that is yet, but it's going to be great.*

She got up, found her abandoned cup of tea and stuck it in the microwave to reheat, realising that perhaps for the first time, she'd given herself a pep talk rather than basically telling herself to *shut up, not feel anything, not complain.* It had been cathartic, yelling at Nathan again. *Perhaps yelling was what I've been missing, all this time. Who knew?*

Chapter Twenty-Two

Lila watched as Maude unwrapped a wicker baby basket stuffed with white baby-gros and nappies.

'You won't believe how fast you'll go through those!' Simona, the hairdresser, called out, holding a half-drunk champagne flute. She was perched on the arm of Maude's floral sofa, and Mara sat next to her.

'Oh, you're so generous, Simona. Thank you!' Maude blushed a little, looking at all the brightly wrapped presents around her. 'I really do appreciate you all being here.'

There were twelve women at the baby shower; Lila stood towards the back of the room, shyly, being polite but not getting too involved. It was good to have something to take her mind off her argument with Nathan, which was a few days ago but was still bothering her.

It had been a perfectly nice Sunday afternoon: they'd all had salmon and dill sandwiches, prepared by Maude on her super soft granary bread from the bakery, and grilled peppers on a bed of hummus on wheat crackers. Maude had made sweet scones and Simona had brought her famous clotted cream from her family's dairy farm, with strawberry jam and butter for those that wanted it. Lila had made her peanut butter millionaire's shortbread and a tray of cupcakes especially for the party.

'Be grateful you're not having twins.' Mara reached for the champagne bottle and topped up hers and Simona's glasses: Maude was drinking sparkling apple juice. 'Feeding was a nightmare. I tried them on the boob but quite honestly, one baby per boob did not work for me. I know you can do it that way, but bottles were the way forward. For me, anyway. There's so much you hear about breast is best and all that, but don't beat yourself up if it doesn't work, or you don't like it. Bottle feeding is absolutely fine.'

'Oh, I agree,' Simona added. 'I breastfed the first one, but after that, I used formula with the other two. So much easier, and Geoff could do feeds in the night that way. I actually got some sleep!' she laughed.

'Well, we're open to all the options,' Maude said, smiling over at Simon, who had just come in with a pot of tea and a tray of mugs. 'The main thing is that the baby's healthy. Being an older mum, you know, we were quite anxious to get beyond the first twelve weeks. I know there can still be complications, but at least that's the first hurdle over with.'

Lila slipped past Simon, who was sorting the mugs on the table.

'Just popping to the ladies.' She pulled the lounge door closed after her and stood outside it with tears in her eyes. This is what she'd dreaded: someone would mention *complications* and it would set her off like some pathetic, weak, snivelling Victorian woman. *Pass the smelling salts*, she thought to herself. *Come on.*

She walked down the hall and into the downstairs bathroom. Maude's house was one of many workmen's cottages in Magpie Cove which dated from the 1880s, built to house the clay workers that had once worked for a bone china factory, now just another part of local history. Lila remembered Maude telling her that the cottage had had an outside privy until the early 1950s. Thankfully, now, everything was modern inside, though they'd kept the working fireplaces.

Lila closed the door to the bathroom, sat down on the toilet and started to cry in earnest. *What is wrong with me?* she thought, angrily, wanting to stop crying, but she couldn't. All the pain washed through her again, making her retch, making her want to scream. She pushed one of the guest towels Maude had in a pile on top of a dresser into her mouth and sobbed, not wanting to be heard.

There was a knock on the door.

'Lila? Are you in there?' Maude's voice came through the door. 'Are you all right?'

Oh, no.

'I'm okay,' Lila croaked, knowing she sounded anything but.

'Lila? What is it? You sound terrible. Are you ill? Can you open the door?' Maude called through the door. Lila felt terrible. She was ruining Maude's baby shower, but she couldn't help it. She shouldn't have come. She knew she shouldn't have. She should have made up an excuse.

'No, I just need a minute,' Lila called out weakly. 'I'm okay, honestly.'

She blew her nose.

'All right… take your time. If you're sure,' Maude sounded doubtful. 'I'll stay here for a minute if you need me.'

Lila tried to take in a deep, calming breath, but Maude being kind just made it worse. She started sobbing silently. She heard Maude sigh, and then her friend's footsteps walking away, down the hall, after a minute or so.

She couldn't go back in that room. Lila knew she looked terrible – she stood up and looked at herself in the mirror. Her face was red and puffy and her eye make-up had run. She clenched the edge of the sink grimly and made herself focus. Okay. If she wasn't going to go back to the party, then she had to leave, as quickly as possible. She knew her handbag was in the hall, and that there was a back door in the kitchen she could leave from, walk around the side of the house and she'd be on the street. No one had to know. She could just text Maude later and say she'd felt suddenly unwell and went home.

She listened at the door. She could hear the party in the front room, but otherwise it seemed quiet in the house. She snicked the door open, checked that the hall was clear, grabbed her bag and made her exit. As she ran down Maude's street, she knew she should go back and explain, but all her instincts – the ones she'd honed from years of looking after herself, at boarding school, in London with Tim – kicked in. *This isn't something we talk about,* she repeated in her mind, as she half ran, half walked along the street, filled with shame. *This isn't something we talk about.*

Chapter Twenty-Three

'Hello.'

Nathan walked up behind her and placed a tentative hand on her shoulder. She jumped: she'd been so lost in her thoughts that she hadn't heard him. 'Beautiful, isn't it?' he asked.

It was a Sunday, a week after Maude's baby shower. She'd seen Nathan at the café here and there when he'd popped in, but he'd definitely been around less, and she'd pretty much ignored him whenever he had come in. She'd worked a week of her notice already, and she'd found a flatshare. It was tiny, on the edge of St Ives, but it would do. One more week of her and Nathan politely ignoring each other and this phase of her life would be over. He'd tried to talk to her on numerous occasions about the rent, but she cut him off each time. What point was there in talking about it now? She'd also been avoiding Maude since the party. She'd texted and made an excuse about feeling ill, and she hadn't been in the bakery since.

'Hello.' She looked away, annoyed that her peace had been interrupted, and incensed that it was Nathan that had apparently sought her out. This was *her* place. The place she came to be alone and think – never mind the fact that soon she wouldn't live nearby and wouldn't be able to just walk up here when she pleased. She'd be able to take scenic views around St Ives, of course, but St Ives was always packed with tourists. She'd be lucky to find a deserted cliff path anywhere there.

He took a few gulps from his water bottle. Lila noted he was dressed in a tracksuit and trainers. His hairline was damp, and a few black curls fell into his eyes. It suited him to look a little rumpled: wild, even. As if the Cornish coastline was having some kind of *Poldark* effect on him. She looked away, back at the view in front of her, and the scattered rock that was edged with wild flowers. *Nathan DaCosta is not a tousled romantic hero*, she scolded herself. *Far from it.*

'This is some view. You come up here a lot?'

'A few times a week, unless the weather's really terrible.' She gazed at the horizon. 'It's peaceful up here. Sometimes I see a few dog walkers, but not that many. Lots of days there's no one else up here but me,' she said, pointedly. She was still furious with him.

'I didn't know you'd be here today, it's a public path,' he said, shortly.

'That's true – I don't own it. Though you might. How much rent is it paying you? Hope it's enough,' she snapped.

There was a silence.

'I used to come up here when I was a kid.' Nathan wiped his arm over his forehead and ran his fingers through his wayward curls, pushing them back. 'When I wasn't away at school. We were the only non-white kids in the village. Used to get called names a lot.' He scowled and kicked a stone. 'Ancient history.'

'I'm sorry about that.' Lila put her hands in her pockets. 'But I'm still angry with you.'

'I know,' he replied quietly. There was another silence: she didn't know what to say. What could she say? It was all done and dusted now.

'Where's your dad now?' she asked, instead. She didn't want to talk but couldn't help feeling curious.

'Dead. He was an alcoholic,' Nathan stated mechanically.

'I remember Serafina telling me they got divorced.'

'Yeah. We didn't see him much after that. He died a few years back.'

'I'm sorry,' Lila repeated. There was another silence.

'I went to boarding school because both my parents died,' she said, breaking the pause between them. 'I was lucky to go.' It would be just like Nathan to complain about being so privileged. *Oh, my diamond shoes are too tight*, she thought, meanly.

'I didn't know that.' He looked at her sympathetically.

'I didn't tell you. How could you?' she shot back. 'The point is, don't complain about the fact you were privileged enough to go to a school that automatically gave you better chances in life than most. You became a successful banker who now gets to be a money-grabbing landlord.' If Nathan DaCosta was in the mood to feel sorry for himself, she wasn't sympathetic. Losing parents was one thing. She'd done that and managed not to victimise the poor as a result.

'Yes, that – and I was good at numbers, an investment bank did a recruitment drive at my school and I got a job there. I worked myself up the ranks,' he replied, evenly. 'And you must know that Mum hadn't raised any rent in fifteen years or more. She was basically a charity. All I've done is bring rents in line with current rates—'

'You told me that already. It doesn't mean anything. It's still your choice,' Lila replied curtly, wishing he'd leave her alone. She let out a breath. 'Look. I can well imagine that your mum and dad must have had it hard, being the only people of colour in the village.' Lila thought of Serafina and her kindness, her way with people. How loved she was. 'But if there was prejudice against her, she certainly turned it around over the years. I've never known anyone who was more a hub of their community. She cared. She knew people were struggling around here. You're making people homeless! Your mum would never have let that happen!'

'It's a business decision,' Nathan snapped. 'It's not personal.'

'For goodness' sake, Nathan! Can you hear yourself? People's homes are personal!'

There was a silence; Nathan paced around the cliff top, going up to the edge and looking over. Lila followed him, alarmed.

'It's all right. I'm not going to jump. Not today, anyway.' He stepped back and turned to her with a half smile.

'Yes, well… if you could do it on your own time, I'd appreciate it.' Lila raised an eyebrow. 'Are you even going to stay in Magpie Cove?'

'I don't know. I didn't think so…' he trailed off.

'Don't you need to go back to the bank? I mean, if they've given you compassionate leave or you've taken holiday, it won't last forever.'

'No,' he said, shortly.

'No?'

'I don't need to go back to the bank,' he added, reluctantly.

'Don't you work for them anymore?' Lila frowned, confused.

'No,' he repeated. His smile had disappeared, replaced by the emotionless mask she hated.

'Well, I guess it's none of my business.' Lila took a deep breath. 'I should probably head on to the next cliff. Leave you to it. As I said, I'll be out of the flat by the end of the month.'

His hand gripped her forearm. 'Lila. Stop.'

'Please don't grab me.' She shook her arm free and glared at him. 'Who do you think you are?'

'I'm sorry. I… I was sacked. From my job at the bank.'

She regarded him coolly. 'You don't need to tell me.'

Nathan refused to meet her eyes, seeming fascinated by the sandy path under his designer trainers. 'I guess the whole experience has… made me lose confidence in my own decisions.' He paused. 'I'd worked at the bank fifteen years. Started after university, which they paid for. Did my MBA, also funded by them. I was practically part of the furniture. And then, I presented some analysis that turned out to be less than perfect.' He took in a deep breath. 'We lost money because of it. A lot of money.' He met Lila's gaze: she saw shame there.

'And they sacked you?'

He nodded.

'That doesn't seem very caring. You worked there all that time. You must have made them lots of money before then.'

'Yes, but that's not how they saw it. It was part of a "performance review" and they basically told me my performance was cause for concern, and they had to let me go because of some restructuring.'

'That sounds like an excuse.'

'Of course it was. I mean, they paid me off pretty well, but being sacked is being sacked. So here I am.'

'I'm sorry. I had no idea. But it doesn't change the fact that what you did here was wrong.'

'Was it? I don't know. Maybe I'm still trying to be a good banker. Make banker decisions. I'm in this limbo and I don't know what to do next. And I don't trust my instincts anymore. I did, for years. I had good instincts. Now...' he trailed off, giving her an intense stare. 'Now, I don't trust my gut anymore. I asked the company that manages the property portfolio to do a flat percentage raise across all the properties. They advised an amount. I didn't know who the tenants were. I didn't know about you, or any of them. I didn't trust myself to get any more involved than that. I didn't trust my feelings about anything. Or... anyone.' He gave her a meaningful look. 'Lila, I've been trying to tell you. You've got to believe me. I would never have pushed you out of Magpie Cove on purpose. I... I thought it was all just business.'

'Well, it wasn't,' she snapped.

Lila felt a knot form in her stomach, thinking about what he'd said about his feelings. *What did that mean?* That Nathan still had feelings... for her? There had been moments when she liked Nathan DaCosta. But they had been destroyed by all the bad things he'd done.

'Please forgive me, Lila. I made some huge mistakes, coming here, taking everything over. You told me weeks ago about the café and I didn't listen. You were right – about the reviews, about all the changes I made. I just thought I knew better, and I didn't. I'm sorry,' he repeated. 'You must think I'm a terrible person.'

'Look, I don't… I mean, I'm sure you thought you were doing the right thing,' she began, not sure what to say. It was diplomatic at best, an outright lie at worst. Lila had definitely spent quite a lot of time thinking Nathan was a pretty bad person.

'It's fine. I… perhaps I shouldn't have said anything, but I don't want you to think I don't care about your job and the café, and the old ladies. I do. It's just…' He put his hands over her his eyes and rubbed his face: it was a gesture of tiredness. 'I was trying to do the best I can for Mum, but now you think I'm some kind of scum landlord. Mum didn't draw anything like a living salary for herself. She ran the café and those properties like a charity.' He shook his head. 'I want the café to be able to stay open. I can see how important it is to people. But I don't know how to run a café, and I don't know how to be her. I've already lost the only thing I know how to do. I realised you were right about the café when you shouted at me that day about the online reviews. But I didn't know how to say it. I'm… not great at admitting I'm wrong.'

Lila snorted. 'Really? I hadn't noticed.'

'Oh, come on. I tried!' he argued. 'I don't think you know how unapproachable you can be. You're so… closed off in yourself, sometimes.'

'You didn't try that hard. We've been working together for weeks since then,' Lila snapped.

'I know, I know. I've been trying to find a way to tell you. There were a few times I walked in, knowing what I was going to say, but you just gave me this withering look and I lost all confidence. I actually came up here to see if I'd run into you. So I could explain.' Nathan took in a deep breath and let it out. 'At least I've done that, anyway.'

'I suppose so,' Lila admitted, grudgingly. She had never imagined that she could be so forbidding from the outside. Yes, she tended to hide her feelings, but she'd always thought she did a good job of appearing neutral and pleasant. *Apparently not.*

He held out his hand. 'Friends?' he asked.

She took his hand; Lila didn't feel right shaking it, so they stood awkwardly hand in hand for a moment.

'Friends,' she agreed.

'This is awkward. We should maybe hug it out,' Nathan suggested.

'Okay…' Lila was surprised that she stepped into the hug almost instinctively. Part of her wanted to kick Nathan DaCosta in the shins, but part of her also wanted to hold him tight and never let go.

They stood on top of the cliff overlooking Magpie Cove, the sea birds flying over them and the sun on their skin. Nathan rested his head on hers, which lay against his chest. Lila was ashamed to admit to herself that she was aware of his hard muscle under his black tracksuit top. Up close, the smell of him was part faint woody aftershave and part fresh sweat, and it was doing things to her. She stepped back slightly, her arms still around his neck and gazed up at him. He met her eyes, and for a brief moment, desire connected them in a crackling current.

What is happening? Lila pulled away from the hug abruptly. Nathan stepped away too, looking embarrassed.

'Sorry. I just… it just felt like the right thing to do.' His words came out in a rush. *Why did I just hug him?* she berated herself. *I didn't have to. I could have said no.* And what was *that?* Lila's knees felt like they might give out on her. She cleared her throat and flexed one knee, and then the other.

'Anyway. Better get going.' She gave him a tight smile.

'Lila, I… I shouldn't have…' his words trailed off.

'It's fine. Don't apologise.'

'I know. I wish you'd reconsider staying. I need someone like you.' He gave her another intense look. 'To make sure the café's run right, I mean,' he added hastily. 'I should have asked you for your ideas some time ago.'

'I gave you my ideas. You just didn't listen,' she reminded him.

'I know,' he replied glumly.

She started walking along the cliff path, and Nathan walked with her, which she didn't quite expect. Oddly, although she hadn't thought Nathan could bare his soul in the way he had, Lila felt something had shifted between them. There was a human being lurking under Nathan's controlled exterior, after all.

'I can't stay, Nathan. I've told you. I can't afford the rent.' Lila took in a deep breath of the sea air; her gaze travelled across the cliffs. 'Maybe it's just time to move on, anyway.'

'What if I lower your rent? And give you a raise at the café?' He reached for her hand. 'Please, Lila. Please reconsider?'

She looked in surprise at their interlinked hands and felt the familiar energy pulsing between them.

'That's a very nice offer. But this isn't just about me. This rent rise affects so many people. I can't forgive that, or the way you did it.' She pulled her hand away. 'I'm sorry, Nathan. I think it's best if I go.'

'I can't promise anything, but I obviously haven't gone about this in the right way. If I review the situation – all the rents – will you consider staying?' he appealed to her. Lila was about to answer when her gaze caught some movement on the cliffs.

'Hey. What's that?' She pointed to a shape that was moving along the cliff side. It reminded her of the day she had seen the mystery climber on the rocks and had almost called the coastguard. 'Oh, no. I think that's a person, isn't it?'

Nathan followed where Lila was pointing.

'Yeah. I think so. But I can't see any guide ropes.' He squinted into the distance. 'That's not a great idea. Free climbing is hard at the best of times, but Magpie Point isn't somewhere you should ever really do that. The tide can be unpredictable even in the summer. One big wave can knock you right off.'

He started walking quickly to the point in the rock where Lila had watched the climber, weeks before. She had a sudden burst of intuition and ran after him.

'Hey. Was that you? Climbing here a few weeks ago?'

'I climb here sometimes, yes.' He was taking his jacket off and handed it to her. 'Call the coastguard. They don't look like they're in control. They might not even be a climber. You can fall onto the ledge and get stuck there.' He pointed down to the think lip of rock she had watched him stop on and climb up from before.

'I don't have the coastguard number. I think it's on that information board back at the top,' Lila panicked.

'Just emergency services will do. They'll pass the call over.' Nathan started running as they both heard a cry from down the rock. 'I'm going to see if I can get down there.'

'Okay. I'm calling.' Lila punched the number into her phone and pressed the call button, running after Nathan. Her heart was in her throat. She was also, behind her panic, mildly annoyed that it had been Nathan all this time that had caused her to worry that day up on the cliffs.

Lila watched, the phone to her ear, as Nathan shouted across the ridge of the cliff to the person below. She could only half hear what he was saying because of the ringing phone in her ear and being slightly out of breath, but she could see he was trying to reassure the climber.

The emergency services operator answered and Lila concentrated on marshalling her thoughts to explain where she was, and that Nathan was trying to rescue the person on his own.

The operator reassured Lila that she would send a helicopter and a boat as soon as possible, but they had already been called out further up the coast an hour ago and the closest helicopter in range would have to come from Plymouth. In the meantime, the operator told her that Nathan should definitely not try to rescue the climber himself.

Lila watched as Nathan scrambled down the side of the rock. 'I'll tell him,' she said, and ended the call.

Lila ran to the edge of the cliff and peered over fearfully. Nathan was making his way down the jagged, fearsome ledges of rock: thank goodness for once he didn't have a suit on, and was actually wearing suitable clothes. Below Nathan, she could see a teenager huddled on the outcrop, leaning back from the edge and hanging onto the rock face behind him. Nathan called out softly to him; as he looked up in surprise, Lila recognised the kid's face. It was John, Mara's son.

'Oh, no,' she breathed. What could have possessed a thirteen-year-old boy to climb down the rock? John seemed to be getting in trouble all the time right now. Lila's memory flashed back to the birthday party and the gossiping mothers. Even if he was being bullied or was in with the wrong crowd, what would induce the boy to climb here on his own?

Below them, the sea crashed onto the rocks. Lila looked away as a flash of vertigo made her nauseous. It was a long and lethal fall if John or Nathan lost their footing. 'Nathan! What are you doing? Be careful!' she called down, unnecessarily. Nathan certainly knew the dangers, and even if John had thought he'd be safe going down, he knew for sure now that he wasn't.

Lila called Mara, her heart pounding. The other woman answered, laughing. Lila's heart tugged in pain, knowing she had to break awful news.

'Hello? Oh, sorry – hello? Who's speaking?'

Someone was in the background, talking to Mara. Lila quickly explained why she was calling. Mara swore; the tone of her voice changed in a second from carefree to terrified; she shouted at the person in the background to be quiet. Lila told her that she'd called 999 and that she was watching Nathan scale Magpie Point right now to get to John.

'I'll be there in ten minutes,' Mara replied, panic obvious in her voice, and hung up.

By now, Nathan had got to John. They were talking; Lila guessed that Nathan was trying to reassure the boy. She watched as Nathan put a protective arm across John's chest. There was no room to sit down and little room to turn around.

'Help'll be here soon!' she shouted down, not knowing if they'd hear her. She wished she had some length of rope with her that she could drop down to them or something. Why wasn't there some kind of bunker with emergency ropes in, in case this happened? Why weren't the cliffs fenced off to stop people falling or climbing over the edge? And what on earth was John doing there at all?

Time slowed to a crawl. Lila waited, not taking her eyes off John and Nathan. Then, she paced up and down for what seemed like an age until a car appeared some way down the road and Mara got out, followed by Brian.

Mara ran to Lila and past her, peering over the side of the cliff.

'Oh my God. John! John! I'm here!' she yelled over the side. She turned to Lila. 'How long has he been down there?'

'I don't know. I called 999, they're sending the helicopter rescue team. Nathan's down there with him.'

'Nathan?'

'Yeah. We were here, walking, and we saw John on the cliff. Nathan climbed down. I guess to reassure him or help provide a bit of safety.' Lila didn't know whether to hug Mara or what else to say. 'I'm sorry. We ran over as soon as we saw him,' she repeated.

'How the hell did he get down there? Brian, can you go down and get him?' the frantic mother appealed to her partner.

'I don't think that would help anyone; I've probably only climbed once or twice.' Brian held Mara to his chest and looked carefully over the side of the cliff. 'Has Nathan got climbing experience? Does he know what he's doing, at least?'

'I think so. But he doesn't have ropes.' Lila looked up at the sky, willing the helicopter to arrive.

'Call Bill, or someone else with a boat. At least they can be there if…' Mara's face screwed up and voice began to wobble. 'Oh, John… Brian, please…'

'I'll call Bill now.' Brian got out his phone and turned slightly away. 'At the museum. He's got a boat,' he explained to Lila, listening for someone to answer at the end. Lila nodded. She knew Bill a little; he sometimes came into the café. He was the picture of a Cornish fisherman: white beard, faded blue cap, usually wearing a cable knit jumper and work trousers with lots of pockets. He always gave Lila a polite *mornin'* or *evenin', maid* when he saw her in the street too, but not much more: a man of few words.

'Right.' Her stomach tightened, understanding what was being implied: if John and Nathan fell, if a boat was there, it could rescue them before it was too late. But it wouldn't stop them hitting one of the rocks submerged under the water. Lila swallowed, feeling her throat thicken in fear.

'Call his climbing instructor too!' Mara yelled. 'See if he can get up here with ropes.' She went to the side of the cliff and lay down on the tussocky grass so that she was looking over the edge; Lila followed her, feeling useless. She wished she could do something.

'John! Mum's here. Sweetheart, why…? How did you get down there? I love you. Help's on the way, okay?' Mara called, fear cracking her voice.

Nathan looked up briefly; Lila could see the tension etched in his face. The boy, John, seemed frozen in shock, but the wind was battering the rock. Lila thought it must be hard to hold on: she wondered how much longer John and Nathan had. Nathan could possibly climb back up without a rope, but not with John too.

The choppy noise of a distant helicopter made Lila look up. *Thank goodness,* she breathed to herself as the rescue team approached. Instinctively she shielded her eyes and stood up to watch it approach.

'Oh thank God, thank God.' Mara sat up and watched it come, her hands clasped together. Brian got off the phone and knelt behind her, encircling Mara in a tight hug. He was repeating, *it's going to be okay, it's going to be okay, I've got you,* but Lila could see in Mara's eyes that her son was the only person she was thinking about.

The helicopter hovered overhead; Lila grabbed Mara and Brian and they ran down the coast path to give the helicopter space to land, slightly away from the noise, hands over their ears. Time remained slow, counted by the rhythm of the helicopter's blades through the air. Lila stood slightly apart from Brian and Mara, feeling a familiar grief rear up again; she knew what Mara felt. She felt the dread of the dream that she knew so well – a fear that was as black as the sea at night. She closed her eyes and begged anyone or anything that was listening to save Nathan and John; not to let another mother lose her child.

Chapter Twenty-Four

Nathan's eyes fluttered open.

'Where am I?' He coughed, wincing.

Oh thank God. Whoever was listening, thank you, thank you. Lila closed her eyes for a brief second, feeling gratefulness wash through her like rain after a heatwave.

'Hospital.' Lila leaned towards him, wanting to do something helpful but not knowing what. Wiping his brow seemed unnecessary.

'I hate hospitals,' he croaked.

'Have some water.' She poured some into a cup from the jug a nurse had left next to the bed and handed him the cup. 'Hang on. Let me adjust the bed a bit.'

She'd been sitting there all night, watching him. The helicopter rescue had been dramatic. The rescue team had lowered a man from the hovering helicopter, who had tied rescue ropes around John and Nathan and took their place on the rock while they were winched to safety. The team in the helicopter had then repeated the process with their team member, and deposited all three of them on the top of the cliff. They'd landed the craft a little further back onto the open moor that covered the top of the cliffs and came to assess John and Nathan.

Nathan, while he was being pulled up, had swayed unexpectedly in a sudden wind and hit his head on the rock. John had hurt his leg on the way down – it seemed that he had started to climb down and then fallen, miraculously ending up on the rock ledge. Other than that, he was just in shock.

Lila pressed the button that raised the back of the bed up. Nathan sipped at the water and winced.

'Thanks.'

'I hate hospitals too. I think everyone does.' Lila looked around at the ward, at the busy nurses, the light green walls. 'You forget how noisy they are,' she added. The beeping machines made her flinch. It was all too familiar. She'd had to spend a night in the London hospital after the miscarriage: they'd said it was common, to have what she had. Sometimes when you lost a baby, not everything came out of its own accord. Just a standard procedure, they'd told her at the time. It didn't feel very standard to her.

'Do you feel okay?' she asked. 'Well, I mean, I know you must be in pain. Stupid question.'

'I'm all right.' He closed his eyes. 'Worst headache I've ever had, though.'

'They've done an MRI or a CT scan or whatever they call it. No brain damage, just a mild skull fracture. It'll heal.' Lila put her hand on his arm. 'You were pretty out of it for that part.'

'I don't even remember. They must have given me some strong drugs.' Nathan blinked hard a few times. 'You were here? All night?'

'Of course. Where else would I go?'

'You must be tired.'

'Well, you're a hero. Least I can do.' Lila took his cup of water and placed it on the table next to the bed. 'If you hadn't climbed down the cliff, John would have fallen before the coastguard got there.'

'Have you seen him? Is he okay?' Nathan tried to sit up straighter and winced. 'Ow.'

'Not yet. They brought us in separate ambulances. But he seemed all right when we were up on the cliff top. Just cold and tired. Upset. Poor thing. He's just a kid.'

'What a nightmare for Mara,' Nathan said. 'I'm glad he was okay. When we were down on the cliff, he just kept repeating he was sorry, his mates had dared him to go looking for fossils in the cliffs. He was too scared not to.'

The relief was intense. She'd sat next to Nathan's bed all night, hardly daring to leave. What if he'd died, or had a serious brain injury?

'Poor kid. I feel terrible. I was intending to tell Mara about John being in the café with those boys – remember, that day you came in and scared them off? Some mums at the birthday party I catered for were gossiping that he's been unhappy about his dad getting a new girlfriend. Acting up. I should have told her, but I got kind of caught up in my own stuff.'

Nathan sighed. 'It's not your fault. Boys can be horrible to each other. I hope he finds some better friends.'

'Me too.'

'I didn't think I'd be back here so soon.' Nathan closed his eyes.

'After Cyd and Betty? I really appreciated you being here with me then. It's only fair I should stay with you in return,' Lila replied.

'Well, that. But I meant Mum.'

'Oh. Of course, Sorry.' Lila kicked herself for having forgotten: they'd brought Serafina here after her heart attack. It had happened at night, so the first Lila had heard had been when she went to work the next morning and found the café closed. 'I came to see her too, but she wasn't awake. She died a few days after I visited.' Lila felt tears spring to her eyes. 'I didn't see you here then.'

'By the time I found out there wasn't long left. I got here on the last day.' Nathan closed his eyes; Lila saw pain clench his face. 'I said goodbye, but I don't think she could hear me.'

'Oh God. I'm so sorry, Nathan.' Lila bowed her head. 'That was both heroic and stupid, what you did on the cliffs today, you know. If she was still here, she'd tell you that.'

'I guess we'll never know what she would have said,' he sighed. 'I miss her.' His voice broke. 'Ah, I've made such a mess of everything. I wish I could see her one more time. Tell her I loved her. That she was right about everything. I was wrong.'

'I miss her too.' Lila felt a tear roll down her cheek and wiped it away self-consciously. 'She was a good friend. I… I'd had a bad time before I got to Magpie Cove and without Serafina, I… I don't know if I would have stayed.' Lila wrapped her arms around her middle.

'What happened? Before you came here?' He turned his head on the pillow and rested his eyes on her. 'I always got the feeling there were things you weren't talking about. Not that you would, to me, anyway. But when I came to your flat you said something about Magpie Cove saving your life, and I wondered what you meant.'

'Um. I… I guess you could say I had a bad break-up.' Lila felt herself automatically reverting to the self-effacing privacy she was so used to, and suddenly she hated it. She'd wanted to tell someone about what happened to her for so long, and here was someone who would listen. Who seemed to care. *You have to trust someone, sometime*, she told herself. He waited, letting her have the space to talk.

'I… I lost a baby. I didn't know I was pregnant, it wasn't something we'd planned, it wasn't something I'd ever even want with him. My ex. But it happened, and it was… I thought I was over it, but…' She felt the tears well up again; her throat got tight. 'I'm sorry. I shouldn't make this all about me.'

Nathan reached for her hand. 'Come on. We know each other better than that now, I hope. I told you some pretty personal stuff up on that cliff. You can tell me.' He touched the bandage around his head. 'I probably won't remember tomorrow, anyway.'

Lila laughed, and then sniffed. 'You don't want to hear it,' she said, wanting to tell him everything, but scared of how it might make him see her. Some kind of loser, maybe someone that couldn't have children. It was irrational – they had chemistry, she couldn't deny that – but they'd never even talked about being together romantically. Yet, the feeling that she was somehow less of a woman for having lost the baby held her back.

'I want to hear it. If it helps you to talk about it,' he said quietly.

Lila took a deep breath, aware of her hand in his and the mutual warmth of their skin. There was that same buzzing feel again, that *rightness* that happened when they touched. It was reassuring. It made her feel strong.

'I left London. After… the miscarriage.' She felt her voice waver again, but Nathan squeezed her hand. She took a deep breath. 'I came to stay with my aunt in Devon, and I heard about the patisserie course. I'd done a lot of other courses and stuff in London in that last year or so. I hated my job.'

'Recruitment, wasn't it? I seem to remember thinking you seemed entirely unsuited to something like that.'

'Like you and banking?'

'Right.'

'So I had to find somewhere to live, and I heard that Magpie Cove was a good place. Your mum kind of took me under her wing. She gave me a part-time job and she found me my flat. Which I now realise was only affordable because it was her property and she set a low rent. Serafina made it possible for me to get on with my life. A new life that was – is – the best I've ever had.'

Nathan nodded and closed his eyes.

'I think this is the first time I've ever been grateful for my mother's obsession with charity,' he replied: there was a smile in his voice, even though he sounded tired. 'Sorry. I don't mean you're a charity case. I mean… I'm grateful she took you in.' He shook his head, then stopped suddenly. 'Ow. It really hurts when I do that.'

'Then don't do it,' Lila chided him gently. She looked away for a minute, thinking. 'I've pushed Maude away, because of her baby. I didn't – I don't – know how to talk to her about it. Because of the miscarriage. I know all the things you're supposed to say and do, and I want to do them. But ... it's just hard, you know? And I don't know why. It's not like I ever planned to have a baby in the first place. I behaved so badly at her baby shower—'

'Humans aren't logical creatures. If they were, life would be so much easier.' Nathan sighed. 'You feel what you feel. You should talk to Maude again. She's your friend, she'd understand.'

'Maybe.' Lila felt pathetic. 'I just don't know how.'

'We're talking, aren't we? And I'm guessing Maude must be a thousand per cent easier to talk to than me.' Nathan paused. 'Look, I wanted to say, about the rent rises. I'll put them back as they were. You can stay and finish your course. So can Maude, and all the rest. I'll figure out another way to keep the business going.' He sighed again. 'I knew when I came here that I'd made bad business decisions in the past. I thought I could prove to myself I was still some big tycoon. I thought I could show Mum I was right, that she shouldn't have given so much away. Turns out, she knew better than me.'

'She was one in a million.' Lila heard her voice waver; she took a deep breath. 'She knew some things are more important than money.'

Nathan squeezed her hand again.

'Yes, they are, and I can't believe it's taken me this long to realise it. I'm sorry about the baby. I can't imagine how you must feel. But for what it's worth, I believe you'll have others. And you'll be such a great mother one day. When it's right for you.'

Lila felt a sob escape her throat.

'Oh, damn. Don't cry.' He sat up and touched her cheek. She was taken aback at the intimate gesture.

'Hey, Lila. Shhh. I'm sorry, I didn't mean…' he murmured into her hair. His arms held her securely. Lila was overcome with the presence of him; it was both heady and comforting. Instinctively she looked up, and, just as instinctively, he kissed her. The hospital noise died away and there was only Nathan and her, together.

She pulled away. Everything she'd told him made her feel exposed, and the kiss made her confused.

'Didn't you want me to…? I'm sorry, I just thought…' Nathan tried to sit up. 'Sorry. I'm not myself.'

'No, it's fine. I… what's going on between us, Nathan? I just don't really understand where we are. Up on the cliff… and now…' Lila was attracted to him, but just like Nathan she didn't trust her instincts. She's been so wrong about him before – or thought she had. He seemed understanding about the miscarriage, and now, because she'd asked him to, he was reversing the whole rent debacle? How could someone be this changeable? And could anyone so changeable ever be trusted?

'I don't know.' Nathan slowly laid back against his pillows. 'Is it okay not to know? I like you. But I'm also kind of… swimmy… right now.'

'Okay.' She sipped a cup of water. 'Don't worry about it.' *Probably not the best time to talk about our relationship, when he has a fairly serious concussion,* she thought. Instead, she said, 'Who knew that all you had to do was rescue a child from the edge of a cliff to become the local hero, anyway?'

'Hmm.' He looked pale. *I should probably go,* she thought.

'Not putting everyone's rent up would have done it without all that,' Lila added, and sat back in her chair. 'So, you're just going to reverse the whole thing? Just like that?'

'I thought that was what you wanted.' He breathed out slowly, as if that hurt too.

'I did. I do. But it seems a big thing to change just because someone asks you to?'

'I told you. Up on the cliff. I hadn't really looked at the detail. It wasn't just because you asked – I made a mistake.' His head started to loll on the pillow. 'I'm tired, Lila. Come and lie next to me for a while? It's rubbish being in hospital alone.'

'You won't forget? That you've promised to do this?'

She balanced awkwardly next to him on the narrow hospital bed. Nathan closed his eyes and reached for her hand.

'I don't think you'll let me,' he murmured. After a few moments he was asleep.

What now? she wondered. It felt as though so much had happened in the space of a day, but she was still no clearer about where she stood with Nathan DaCosta. All she knew was that she had feelings for him which were difficult to describe. It seemed as though he too had been stung by failure – or, felt as though he had, at least. She felt an odd kinship with him, understanding what it was to project an image of being in control, with your feelings raging underneath. They were the same in so many ways, but was that a good thing?

She could have left, but she stayed next to him on the bed. She didn't quite know why she stayed, only that being near him made her feel safe, even though he was injured and unconscious. And it wasn't just that: Lila realised she felt protective of him. He was so clearly someone who rarely asked for help – like she was – and it made her sad. She touched his face softly, tracing his dark brows and then the roughness of his black stubble. *Two sad souls, too afraid to reach out,* she thought. Even if he didn't know it, then she could be here for him now.

Chapter Twenty-Five

Two months later

'Higher up!' Lila called to Oliver who stood on top of a stepladder, pinning pink paper garlands to the wall of Magpie Cove's Shipwreck and Smuggling Museum.

'If I reach any higher, I'll fall off,' Oliver grumbled. 'Hand me another one.'

Lila passed him a paper chain and scanned the room, which was a hive of activity. 'You look nice.' She gave him a suspicious glance. 'Expecting anyone in particular?'

'Maybe…' Oliver raised an eyebrow and smiled. 'My lips are sealed.'

'Your lips are never sealed.' Lila looked around the room. 'Where's Nathan?' she asked. 'He should have been here half an hour ago.'

'Don't ask me.' Oliver attached the decorations to the old beams of the ceiling and sneezed. 'This place is covered in dust. God knows when it was last cleaned.'

'Well, it's the only place in Magpie Cove big enough to hold a dance party, and I guess Bill doesn't get up to the rafters with a feather duster that often.' Lila passed Oliver some paper decorations in the shape of dancing shoes to hang up. Bill, the elderly part-time curator of the museum, was fiddling with the equally aged generator in the corner. Lila realised that it been he whom Brian had called for help, that day on the cliff. Fortunately, they hadn't needed him after all: she shuddered briefly, imagining Bill having to pull John from the water. Oliver glanced over.

'Hope he's going to change before the dance. Don't think oil-stained overalls are quite the look we're going for,' he whispered loudly.

'Shhh. He's doing us a huge favour.' Lila glared at her friend. 'Finish hanging the decorations. I've got to set the food out.'

At that moment, the fairy lights that Lila had strewn everywhere around the museum blinked on. The old fishing boats and dusty glass cabinets filled with maritime exhibits – stuffed sea birds, sailors' maps, old leather logbooks – suddenly took on a fairy-tale feel. Bill gave a satisfied huff.

'There you go, maid.' He tapped his old blue cap in Lila's direction.

'Oh, Bill, it's lovely.' Lila gazed around her at the museum. Cyd and Betty would love this.

Since they'd been home from the hospital, she and Oliver had been visiting every week, making dinners and bringing cakes. They'd also started visiting Rovina, Eric and a group of six other elderly Magpie Cove residents. She and Oliver were almost at the end of their course, so it had been challenging to fit in all the visits, but worthwhile.

When they'd learnt that it was going to be Betty's eightieth birthday, Lila knew they had to do something special, so they'd arranged this surprise party for her – but also as a treat for Cyd, too. Calling in on all the elders, Lila had learnt so much about their lives and the past – what it was like for Eric, being the only policeman in Magpie Cove until he retired, or for Rovina, growing up in an orphanage after World War Two. Getting to know the community made Lila feel that she belonged, somehow, something she'd never felt before.

Lila was already ready for the evening in a forest green Fifties rockabilly dress with a full skirt, elbow-length sleeves and her waist cinched with a black elasticated belt. The green contrasted beautifully with her curly red hair. Oliver wore a sharp navy blue single-breasted suit, slim and fitted, with a white triangular hand-kerchief in the top pocket and a white shirt with a bolo tie. He'd gelled his hair into a Fifties style blond quiff to match the look.

'Okay. That's all the decorations up.' He approached the corner where Lila had set out three trestle tables covered in lace tablecloths she'd found in a drawer at Serafina's. 'The band is setting up over there.'

Lila cast an eye over to the stage where a rockabilly band were arranging their amps and testing microphones. The singer, a girl with many tattoos up her arms and pink and black hair in a shiny ponytail atop an undercut, wore a pink poodle Fifties skirt and a black tank top. The double bass player waved at Lila from where he was studying some notes and practising some riffs on his black and white painted bass.

'They look amazing. Where'd you find them?' she asked.

'College, would you believe. Turns out that some of our fellow patisserie enthusiasts also play lindy hop in their spare time.' Oliver grinned. 'People'll start arriving soon. You got everything under control, my redheaded Liz Taylor?'

'Yep. Just got to put the food out, wait for Nathan to get here and there's also… aha!' Lila waved at John, dressed in black, walking shyly over to her food table. 'Hey, John. Right on time. Apron for you.'

The teenager nodded and took it.

'It looks great.' He grinned, looking at the decorations. 'I've never even been in here before.'

'Who knew Bill had so much floor space, huh?' Lila gazed around at the museum. 'There are actually some quite interesting exhibits up on the mezzanine. If you're into the fishing history of Magpie Cove. Smuggling too. There are caves around here somewhere, Bill told me, that smugglers used to use. Who knew?'

'Wow.' John looked politely interested.

'Okay, well, maybe not so fascinating when you're thirteen.' Lila grinned.

'Fourteen.' John corrected her. 'It was our birthday last month.'

'Oh, of course.' Lila nodded. 'I'd forgotten. Well, you're so kind to help us out tonight. Basically, if you can replace empty dishes, make sure the older guests get food, clean up as we go, that would be great.'

'No problem,' John said, tying his apron. 'Mum, Franny and Brian are just coming. Mum's doing Franny's hair.'

'Perfect.' Mara was running the bar for the evening. She'd also found a lindy hop dance troupe to come along and demonstrate the dance moves for everyone who had arrived and were doing some practice moves on the dance floor.

'You really roped the community in, huh?' Oliver gave Lila a hug as they stood watching everything.

'Mmm. John's changed so much, don't you think?' She lowered her voice. 'Remember how he was running around with that gang from his school? After what happened on the cliff, I don't know what Mara and Brian did exactly, but he started helping out at the café soon after and I'm pretty sure she made sure the school dealt with the bullying problem. He's a changed kid.'

'Good for him. And Mara and Brian,' Oliver cheered. 'It's so easy to go off the rails as a teen. I got bullied a lot at school when I came out. Fortunately, I had some great friends who stood by me and helped me through it. It was hard, though.'

'I can't imagine anyone ever bullying you.' Lila looked up at her friend. 'You own the room wherever you go.'

'Nowadays, sure – if it's my type of room, anyway. Not all rooms, believe me. I would never have gone into that old man's pub in the village for the first time unless it was with you. You can be as fabulous as you want, but there are still plenty of places that aren't friendly when you're determined not to hide your light under a bushel. As a gay man, that is. As it turned out, Barry the bartender and I have become quite good friends.'

'Why are people so horrible to each other?' Lila sighed. 'I'll never understand it.'

'Who knows? They don't like themselves, usually.' Oliver shrugged. 'Anyway, I'm glad John's turned a corner.'

'Me too.' Lila waved as Mara, Brian and Franny made their entrance. 'Wow. They all look so good!'

Franny's black hair was combed into a high ponytail which made a perfect ringlet down her shoulders. She wore a white full-skirted dress with a white flower corsage on her wrist. Mara looked stunning in a figure-hugging black dress, cut flatteringly to the knee, with a red belt and flat red shoes, her black curly hair recently cut short to show off her high cheekbones.

'Oh my days, it's Rizzo from *Grease*!' Oliver yelled in delight, ran over to Mara, picked her up and twirled her around. 'Miss Mara Hughes, you are looking *fine* this evening! Put me on your dance card, okay?'

Mara bowed theatrically. 'If I get out from behind the bar, I'm all yours.' She grinned. 'Hey, Lila. Great job with all this.'

'I had a lot of help.' Lila came over to hug Mara.

Oliver shook Brian's hand.

'You're looking pretty sharp yourself, Oli.' Brian grinned. 'Wow, this looks great! Magpie Cove really knows how to pull together for a good cause, huh?'

Mara shook her head. 'I just can't believe Nathan's paying for all this.'

'Well, you know, he's changed a lot since the accident,' Lila said, carefully. Nathan had spent a lot of his time away from Magpie Cove in the past months, selling his flat in London and then spending time with his brother James in Jamaica. He and Lila had emailed intermittently: there was something there between them, but after the accident Nathan had left town almost as soon as he was allowed home from the hospital.

He had changed, though, it was true. When she'd mentioned her idea for Betty's eightieth, he'd offered to pay for it immediately and sent her whatever she needed. Their emails had been honest: he had repeated that he really liked her, but he needed time to think.

He'd written, one day:

My whole life has changed, and I guess I thought I was okay with it, but I'm not. Mum passing away has hit me harder than I expected. It's like everything I thought was true about myself is a lie, and the one person I had to depend on is gone.

I know it sounds stupid, but I need time to find myself before I make any decisions affecting other people. I really, really like you, Lila, but I don't want to make a commitment before I'm sure.

He'd unexpectedly come back from Jamaica a week ago, but she hadn't seen him yet. She and Mara had kept the café open while he was away, but Mara had wondered out loud to her more than once whether he was coming back at all. Lila had, privately, wondered the same thing. She'd kept in touch – it felt too important a connection to let it slide – so she'd sent him funny GIFs and messages here and there when there hadn't been an email for a while. At the same time, she realised that it might not happen between them, and she'd tried to rationalise that – with Nathan away, being noncommittal, she should keep her options open too.

She'd even been on a couple of friendly dates. One was with a guy from her course who had always been nice to her, who she liked but wasn't attracted to in the slightest. And there was one blind date that she hadn't even realised was a date until she arrived at Simona Gordon's home for dinner and found the table set for Simona, her hulking-yet-gentle husband Geoff and a single friend of theirs, Paul, a farmer from down the coast. It had been a very pleasant night – apart from Simona's blatant efforts at matchmaking.

Alice had come down to visit for a few weekends too and it had been so good to see her friend again: they'd had a few raucous nights out in St Ives with Oliver and she'd finally been able to relax and let her hair down. As soon as she'd seen Alice step off the train, she'd realised how much she'd missed her – and what an idiot she'd been to push her away all the time she'd been in Cornwall.

'Nathan is supposed to be picking up Cyd and Betty and bringing them here, but he had some business to do in Exeter before. I just hope he isn't going to be late.' Lila looked anxiously up at the rusty vintage clock on the museum wall, which advertised a well-known cough lozenge and a picture of a white-bearded fisherman not dissimilar to Bob himself. 'But yes. I think he has changed.'

'The love of a good woman will do that for you.' Brian smiled fondly at Mara and took her hand. Lila blushed, though she loved how sweet they were with each other.

'Well… maybe. He had a chance to make it up to the community and a party for everyone seemed like a good way to do it,' Lila explained. 'Since he gave up on the time restrictions and the price hikes at the café, reviews have improved again. And especially now we're stocking Maude's cakes again.' Lila waved at Maude, who had sashayed in with her husband Simon. Maude looked delightful and hugely pregnant in peach tulle: like one of her own buns. She came over and enveloped Lila in a hug.

'Hey, sweetie. How are you? You okay? I haven't seen you for a week or so. I've got a baby shower job I need to speak to you about, if you want some extra cash? They've asked me to cater and I could do with another pair of hands.' She let Lila go, but not before giving her a final squeeze. 'I'm so glad we had that talk, you know.'

Lila had drummed up the courage to talk to Maude about why she'd run out on her baby shower and why she'd been so distant after she'd found out her friend was pregnant. She'd sat in Maude's cosy lounge, drinking tea and eating some of Maude's famous iced doughnuts, and been completely honest about everything. And it had helped. Ever since, she'd felt so much lighter. She'd also apologised for being a terrible friend. Not that Maude would accept that she had, of course. Instead, Maude had insisted that Lila go round for dinner once a week with her and Simon, and that, if she wanted to, she love to have Lila's help with the baby once it arrived. Lila found that she was looking forward to it.

More and more locals drifted in; the band started playing some background music and the buzz in the museum got louder and louder. Lila returned to man the food tables with John and peeked at the large cake box that she'd stashed under the table. Her final project for the course had been to create an elaborate event cake, and Betty's birthday cake was a replica of the one she'd just submitted to Jakob this week.

Final marks wouldn't be sent out for a week or two yet, but Lila felt confident.

Inspired by Cyd and Betty's life of dance, Lila had made a huge, perfectly spherical glitter ball cake which, when cut into, featured eight rainbow layers, spiked with rum – Betty's favourite. The glitter ball itself was crafted from two white chocolate hemispheres which had been incredibly difficult not to break, with the cake cut to perfect size inside. The ball was covered in a shiny silver high gloss ganache, and at the centre of the rainbow layers, lay a secret sphere of coconut and lime cream. As part of her submission for her coursework, Lila had written up interviews with Cyd and Betty about their lives together and dance community in Cornwall in the 80s to the present day. Jakob had seemed pleased when she'd carefully handed the cake in, and delighted when she'd invited him along for the evening.

She stood up and felt her phone buzz in her pocket.

We're outside.

It was the agreed message from Nathan, meaning he was outside with Cyd and Betty. Lila tapped John on the arm.

'Back in a minute.'

Lila ran to the closed double doors of the museum, waving at everyone.

'They're here!' she hissed. The room quietened, and Bill turned down the lights.

Lila stepped outside.

Chapter Twenty-Six

'Good evening, ladies.' Lila beamed at Cyd and Betty, though her heart was beating like a drum at seeing Nathan for the first time in two months. She felt unreasonably shy. 'Hi, Nathan,' she added.

'Hello, Lila.' She'd forgotten how smooth his voice was. She felt herself blushing and was immediately mortified.

'Oi! Wot's goin' on, Lilly?' Cyd squinted in the late-summer evening light: this time of year, the sun wouldn't set until ten and the sky was still a deep blue. 'Not that we don't like bein' chauffeured around by a handsome young man, but it's almost time for our radio drama.' Cyd leaned on a walker and Betty on a stick, though she held Nathan's arm.

'Well. A little bird told me that it was a big birthday for Betty,' Lila said innocently, glad of the distraction from an awkward conversation with Nathan. The last time she'd seen him, it was a few days after he'd fallen asleep holding her hand in the hospital. Then, he'd been all business again, telling her that he was leaving to spend time with his brother in Jamaica. What was a good ice-breaker now? *Hope you had a good time with James, how was Jamaica, is there something going on between us now or not because I kind of feel like there was and then you ran away for two months?*

'Follow me,' she said, instead, avoiding eye contact with Nathan.

'What, into the museum?' Betty tsked. 'I'm not in the mood for a tour, my love.'

'Just trust me on this.' Lila beckoned them forward, and they followed, warily.

'Come on.' Nathan led them carefully through the doors, holding them open until both had hobbled through.

'SURPRISE!!!!' everyone called out. Bill flicked the fairy lights and the main lights on, and the band started playing 'Happy Birthday'.

'Happy birthday, Betty!' Lila gave the startled woman a hug, and hugged Cyd too. 'Sorry, Cyd. I knew you'd tell her if I told you.'

'Oh my… Saints alive!' Betty breathed, taking it all in. 'Oh, I can't believe it! Look, there's Eric! Oh, Maude! A band! Bill, were you in on this?'

'Well, I'm flabbergasted,' Cyd gasped, and planted a kiss on Betty's cheek. ''Appy birthday, my darlin'. And thank you, Lilly. This is the nicest thing anyone's ever done for us.' She wiped a tear from her eye.

Lila got them settled in a couple of comfortable chairs and John brought them a glass of champagne each, then placed a little table between them for food. While he did that, Lila took Nathan with her behind the food table, got the cake out of the box and carried it carefully over to the couple. Lila started singing 'Happy Birthday' as they walked, and everyone joined in this time. Lila set the cake down carefully on the table between the women, and lit an '80' candle she'd placed at the top.

'Make a wish,' she whispered to Betty, who gazed up at her in amazement.

'This is for me?' she whispered back, looking quite overwhelmed.

'Of course it's for you.' Lila knelt down next to Betty's chair and took her hand. 'You deserve it.'

Betty took a deep breath and blew out the candle, and everyone cheered.

'Well, if that ain't the most shiny silver ball I ever seen!' Cyd exclaimed, as Lila tapped carefully at the silver-coated chocolate to break it and cut two slices.

'Ooh, it's a rainbow inside!' Betty cooed. The crowd chattered and Lila bowed at some wolf whistles and appreciative cheers. Maude gave her the thumbs up.

'With… lime and coconut ganache.' Lila carefully spooned out a little and added it onto each plate with a spoon. 'Here. From me.'

Nathan and John took the cake back to the food table to cut it into slices for everyone, and Lila crouched down beside Betty as she took a bite. 'How is it?' she asked, a little nervously. Jakob appeared from the crowd and bowed to the ladies.

'*Gut* evening, ladies,' he said, formally. 'And a very happy birthday.'

'Jakob! Cyd, Betty – this is my patisserie teacher,' Lila introduced them.

'My heavens, this is a bloody marvellous cake!' Betty exclaimed, mouth half full. 'Did you teach 'er how to make this, my lad? Best cake I ever had.'

'I did, but ze concept was all her own. Miss Bridges, you are to be highly commended. Your cake voz technically excellent and well-executed, but ze purpose and ze meaning you have incorporated into your project is remarkable.'

'Has she passed, then?' Cyd reached out and poked Jakob in the leg from where she sat. 'Go on, tell us. She's worked so bloody 'ard this year, bless 'er.'

'Vell, I vouldn't normally tell you… but tonight seems a special occasion.' Jakob nodded. 'Oh, good evening, Mr Kay.'

Oliver had danced up to where Cyd and Betty were sitting and planted kisses on each of their cheeks.

'Happy birthday, Betty!' he said between kisses. 'Now, who wants a place on my dance card for the evening, because it's filling up fast.' He cast a glance at a very good-looking tall man with a neatly trimmed black beard who was talking animatedly to a perplexed-looking Bill. 'If you know what I mean.'

'Ooh. Is that the guy you've been dating?' Lila nudged Oliver. 'Very James Bond.'

'I know. And yes.' Oliver beamed. 'Hi, Jakob! Looking sharp.'

'So?' Betty prompted Jakob. ''As she passed, or not?'

'Well, in fact, I can tell you zat you both passed vith distinction.' Jakob nodded at Lila and Oliver. 'You vill receive your official marks next week, but – congratulations!'

Oliver screamed, picked Lila up and twirled her around.

'Oh my… we DID IT!' he yelled. Lila hugged him tight as he lowered her back to the floor.

'Are you serious?' Lila gaped at Jakob. 'We passed? I passed?!'

'You did.' Jakob bowed again. 'And now, I vill go and get some cake for myself. Ladies, a pleasure.' He did a funny little formal wave and left them to join the queue for the food table.

'Oh my goodness. I never thought this day would come!' Oliver breathed. 'Are you okay? You've gone quiet.'

Lila was watching it all: the people dancing, Simon and Maude holding hands, watching the dancing, Brian laughing with a couple of the old men from the pub. She loved Magpie Cove so much. And… *She'd passed.*

'I'm fine. Just taking it in, I guess. No more college. What happens now? I just never thought it would end so soon.'

'No more college!' Oliver squealed. 'I can't believe it. I'm going to tell Eddie.' He hugged her again and kissed her on the forehead. 'Well done, Miss Bridges. After everything you've been through to get here, you deserve this,' he whispered in her ear before running excitedly over to his date.

If her course was over, what was really keeping her in Magpie Cove? She was a qualified patissier. She and Oliver had dreamt of

Michelin-star kitchens, luxury yachts, even being their own bosses, running private catering. But now that it all lay in front of her like a table covered with delicious pastries, what did she want? She didn't want to just work in the café part time anymore. Yet it had been the café that had started it all: it was Serafina, she corrected herself, that had made everything possible for her. Grief tugged at her heart.

She turned around to find Nathan right behind her.

'Oh. Hi!'

'Hi yourself.' He smiled gently down at her.

'I was just thinking, your mum would have loved this,' she said, watching the dancers.

'She would have.'

There was a silence between them as the band played and the villagers tried their hands – and feet – at lindy hop.

'So, how are y—'

'How's things?'

They spoke at the same time, then laughed.

'You first.' Nathan put his hands in his pockets: rather than one of his usual suits, he wore smart brown wide-legged trousers and a retro bowling-style shirt.

'I'm fine. I think this is the first time I've seen you in anything apart from a suit or sportswear.' Lila looked him up and down. 'You look so different! You grew your hair, too.' She wanted to touch the luxurious brown-black curls that he pushed back from his face in a self-conscious gesture.

'I know. I didn't see the point in getting it cut while I was away,' he said, shyly. 'And when you wrote and told me the theme was lindy hop, James helped me find this outfit. We went to this really fun vintage clothes shop in Kingston.'

'You had a good time together?' Lila accepted a glass of champagne from John as he came past with a tray of drinks. 'Thanks, John.'

'We spent some quality time together, probably for the first time ever. Visited my dad's relatives. We talked a lot. About Mum, Dad, our childhood. Everything.'

'I'm so glad.'

'Yeah. Me too. So, I came to some decisions when I was out there. About the business…'

Lila nodded, carefully. *Did you think about me? Because I thought about you,* she thought, but didn't know how to say. *I thought about you every day.*

'The private catering seems to have been going well in my absence. Is that fair to say?'

'Oliver's been really busy. He seems to love it.' Lila smiled, watching her friend, who was dancing slowly with Betty and chattering away, making her laugh.

'But you, not so much?' Nathan turned to her. 'Be honest.'

'Umm… it's fine. I mean, I need the work right now. But no, it's not totally my cup of tea.' She shrugged.

'That's what I thought. Which is why I'm making Oliver the Manager and Head Chef of the private catering business. And, if you're interested, I thought you might like to run something new for me?'

He handed her a folded piece of paper.

'What's this?' She opened it and read it, frowning. 'I don't understand.'

'The café at the end of the street that's been closed, like, forever,' he explained. 'I bought it. Once James and I went through the whole of Mum's estate, we realised it was much more extensive than I'd thought. I made a quick sale of a couple of vacant properties she owned, and bought that one. It needs a bit of renovation, but that's no problem.'

'Another café? I don't understand.' She handed it back to him. 'You have one already.'

'The new premises are for the catering business. Oliver needs a professional kitchen – something more than what we have at the café. We can custom build it there,' he went on. 'And that means that the private catering side of things can subsidise a community café. We keep Serafina's as it is, but we create a pay-what-you-can menu for the vulnerable in Magpie Cove. Cyd, Betty, Eric – all our elderly customers, but the families too. Anyone on the breadline, they can come and get a hot meal from us. And if you want to, I want you to head that up.'

'Me? A community café?' Lila looked at him in amazement.

'You inspired me. You care so much about people here. You did all this. The party. Dressing up as Abba or whoever it was with Oliver to raise money so you could do it yourself. Even stealing food to give Cyd and Betty because you were so worried.' Nathan grinned. 'You proved to me over and over again how much you care about people, but also that you've got…' he clicked his fingers, 'moxie. Isn't that what cool hep cats said in the lindy hop days?'

'Moxie?' Lila was struggling to keep up.

'You know – you're determined. You work hard for what you want. I admire that about you. And, despite our methods being… quite different, I think we've got that in common.'

'Okay.' Lila didn't know what to say. 'Thanks.'

'Anyway, it's something that Mum would like, I think. Just a more formal version of what she already did. With a firmer grasp of sensible accounting.'

'I'd love to do it,' Lila said, thinking. 'But my course… I mean, I came to realise I wasn't interested in catering fancy parties. But I do still love making patisserie. Would a community café let me do that?'

'I don't see why not. Maude is going to be taking a break soon because of the baby, so we won't be able to get our gateaux from her for a while. I thought, also, if you were interested – maybe you and Oliver might run some beginners' baking classes? Lots of people would love to learn. You could even teach me how to make a cake.' He gave her a rueful smile. 'Though I don't think I'd be very good at it. And, you know, rather than me just employing you, we could arrange a way for you to buy in to the business. I want you to be a key part of everything.'

'We could sell what people made in the classes in the café,' Lila suggested. 'As well as my stuff. If that was all right...'

'Of course it would be all right. So is that a yes?' He bit his lip, looking anxious.

Lila gazed around her: at all the people she loved, having a great time at a party she'd organised. This was the place where she finally felt she belonged. Maybe it was the first place she'd ever let anyone in to her heart – Oliver, Cyd, Betty, Serafina – she looked up at Nathan. Yes. Maybe some others, too.

'Yes,' she said. 'I'll do it.'

Nathan whooped and grabbed her in a huge bear hug. 'Lila, I don't want you to leave,' he said. 'You'll stay, won't you? I mean, in the flat. In Magpie Cove?'

'Yes,' Lila murmured against his chest. 'If I can afford to, then that's what I'd always planned.'

'Good. You see, I... *I* want you to stay. For me,' he whispered in her ear.

'Why?' Lila stood back and stared up at him.

'Because I like you,' Nathan whispered. 'Because I liked you from the first day I met you. And for the longest time I couldn't imagine what my life was going to look like after I lost my job in London. I lost the future I'd planned. But now, I can see a future. In Magpie Cove. With you, if you'll give it a go.'

'I like you too,' she whispered as they parted, her heart craving him, to be held in his arms again and never let go. 'When you're not being a cold-hearted capitalist.'

'I hope those days are behind me.' He grinned. 'Well, the cold-hearted part, at least,'

'I do want to stay. I love Magpie Cove,' she said. 'I never wanted to leave.'

'I think we can have everything we want if we just believe we can,' he murmured. 'And I want you, Lila Bridges.'

'Your mum would have told us that there's nothing that we can't achieve,' Lila said, remembering Serafina.

'I'm just sad that she's not here. To be horribly smug that she got us together in the first place.' Nathan rolled his eyes. 'Love conquers all, or something like that.'

'Love?' Lila felt a resounding *yes* in her heart, so strongly that it shocked her. Was this what love felt like? Was this what all Barbra's songs were all about? *I guess so,* she thought.

'I said what I said. Perhaps I'll say it again one day.'

'Perhaps you will,' she replied, her eyes twinkling.

'Look, Lila. All the time I was away, I was thinking about you. And that night in hospital, you told me something very personal. Something difficult for you. And, if I'm honest, I don't remember exactly what I said because I was kind of out of it,' Nathan confessed.

'That's okay. You—' Lila tried to answer.

Nathan interrupted her, squeezing her hands in his. 'Please, let me finish. I've got it all prepared in my head and I need to say it. I promise you'll never have to face anything like the miscarriage alone again. I'm sorry I wasn't there then, to hold your hand and tell you it was going to be okay. But I will be now. And I'll try not to make any more terrible decisions, like leaving you. I want you. For as long as you'll have me, anyway.' He looked at his shoes, shyly. 'That's it.'

'Doesn't you being my boss complicate things?' she asked, wanting to kiss him. She was very aware of how close they were standing together; aware of his body, of the way it felt when he held her to him. She put her champagne glass down on a nearby table.

'I don't know. But I think we should try it and see. You'll be in charge of the café. It's your thing, I'm just the silent owner.' He gave her a deep look. 'A very silent owner that would like to kiss you now.'

Lila stepped forward so that now she was pressed against him. He smiled and leaned in to her. Lila was dimly aware of the noisy party around her: of the music, the laughter, the clink of glasses. But when Nathan's lips met hers, she finally found peace.

A Letter from Kennedy

Hi! I hope you enjoyed *Secrets of Magpie Cove*. If you did enjoy it and want to keep up to date with all my latest releases, just sign up at the following link. Your email address will never be shared and you can unsubscribe at any time.

www.bookouture.com/kennedy-kerr

Many things inspired this story, but two most of all. The first were my great aunts Jean and Marjorie – my grandmother's sister and her long-term partner. Jean and Marjorie were devoted to each other their whole lives, from meeting as nannies in a children's home in their early twenties to their finally passing away in their eighties. They had a life of fun, family, jokes, obsessive board game playing and were really loved in their small village. (They weren't ballroom dancers, but they definitely knew how to party.) I modelled Cyd and Betty on them, as I think it's important for us all to remember – as Oliver says – being gay is not a new thing, even though it may not have been as socially acceptable in the past as it is now. Also, I wanted to write something where the younger characters cared for the older ones and valued their elders for their wisdom and friendship.

The second thing that inspired Lila's experience of miscarriage was Meghan Markle's brave sharing of her experience in 2020, along with the experiences of many other women I know and have known. There remains a terrible stigma about miscarriage and, like many aspects of women's health, it doesn't seem to be something society is comfortable with us talking about. Yet talking about miscarriage and other trauma is essential to help us process it. As Meghan said, asking each other if we are okay, and not being afraid to say 'no', is the first step.

With all my good thoughts,
Kennedy

If you'd like to hear more about my books,
you can find me on Facebook and Twitter:

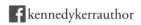 kennedykerrauthor

 @kennedykerr5

Acknowledgements

I used Marcus Wareing's 'lemon, meringue, ice tea' recipe for the scene with Lila and Oliver at patisserie school. You can find it here: www.greatbritishchefs.com/recipes/lemon-curd-dessert-recipe?_ga=2.214949015.1616951264.1605002442-420134235.1605002442

Printed in Great Britain
by Amazon